RED EMPIRE

BOOK II OF THE IMPERIAL CHRONICLES

THE COMING YEARS WOULD TEST THE COURAGE
OF CITIZENS AND SUBJECT PEOPLES, OF
LEGIONARIES AND SLAVES, OF THE MEN AND
WOMEN OF THE EMPIRE; AND DETERMINE
WHETHER THE NATION CHOSEN BY IMPERIUM
WOULD FULFILL ITS CALLING: TO RULE OVER ALL
THE WORLD.

—Primo Alleus, national historian, writer of *The Imperial Chronicles*

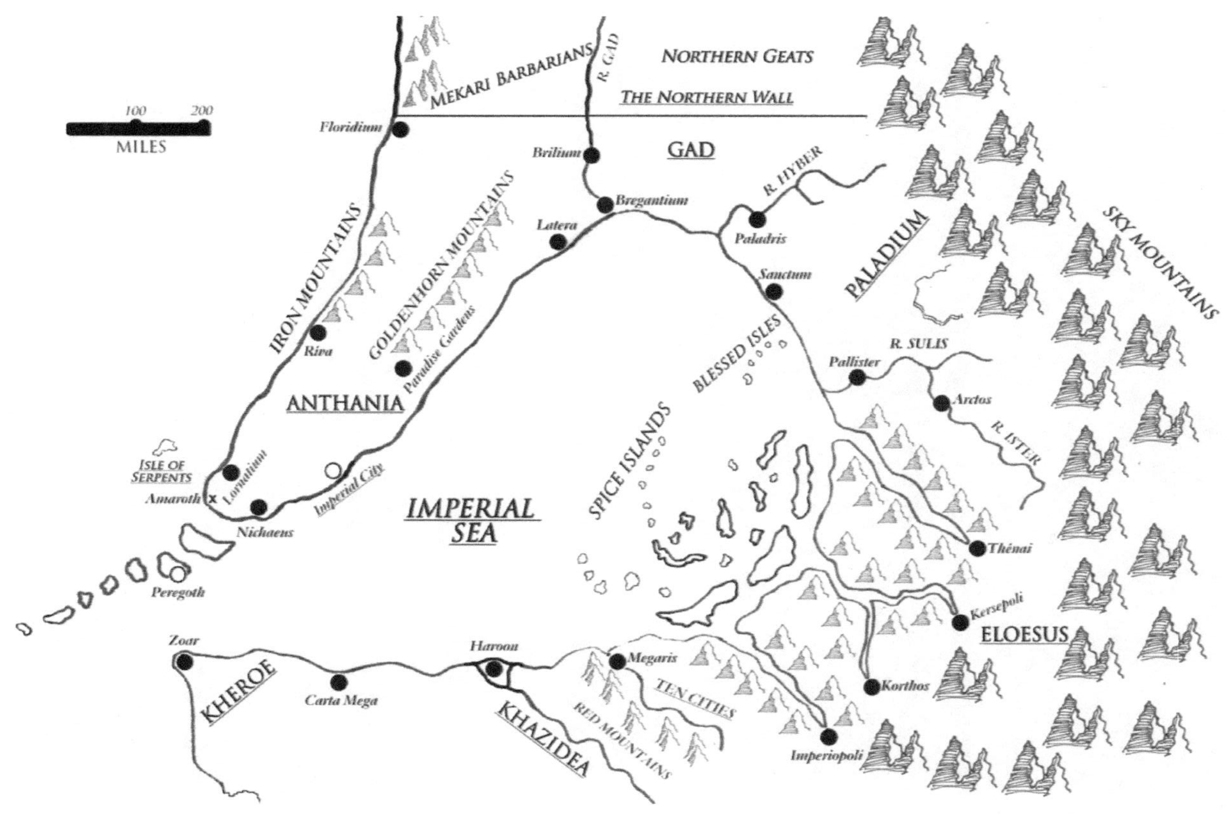
MILES
100
200
NORTHERN GEATS
MEKARI BARBARIANS
The Northern Wall
R. GAD
Floridium
GAD
Britium
Bregantium
R. GAD
Latera
Paladris
Sanctum
PALADIUM
R. HYBER
IRON MOUNTAINS
GOLDENHORN MOUNTAINS
Paradise Gardens
Pallister
R. SULIS
Arctos
R. ISTER
SKY MOUNTAINS
Riva
ANTHANIA
BLESSED ISLES
SPICE ISLANDS
Theimi
ISLE OF
SERPENTS
Amarath
Loriattium
Nichaeus
Imperial City
IMPERIAL
SEA
Kersepoli
ELOESUS
Korthos
Peregoli
Zour
Harou
Megaris
TEN CITIES
Imperiopoli
KHEROE
Carta Mega
KHAZIDEA
RED MOUNTAINS

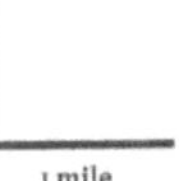

Imperial City

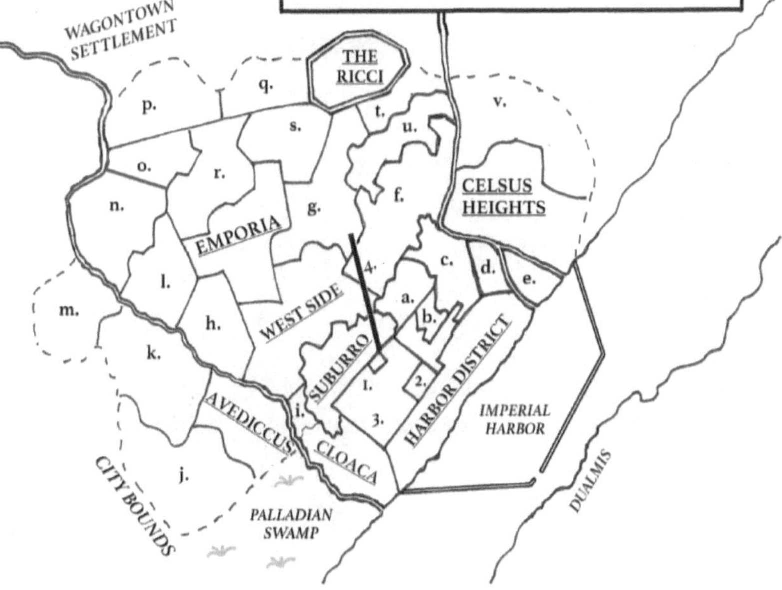

PROLOGUE: BARBARIANS

Masimo Vorenus, Augur

The head of the berserker's axe was large as a chariot-wheel, and it clove clean through the legionary's helmet down to his waist. The berserker himself stood half again the height of the Imperial soldiers, and his blond hair seemed mismatched with his cold black eyes. Huric, they called him. Huric the Giant, Huric the Wild. Masimo guessed he had killed three dozen men already, maybe more.

They were twenty miles from Imperial City, and Imperial City had no walls. They needed a warning before this rampaging barbarian host set the capital of the Empire alight. They'd burst forth from beyond the Wall, torched farms and massacred villagers, and now… now, the legion could not stop them.

An arrow stuck Huric in the shoulder, but he made no sign of noticing. He heaved back his giant axe as his face reddened, and chopped a legionary clean in half. The torso hit the blood-soaked ground, and Masimo whimpered.

A spear pierced Huric's side and blood trickled down his bare white chest, but this only enraged him. He cried out and charged the legionary. Masimo called up the power of Wind, leapt, and let it carry him backward. His insides had turned to jelly, by now. The barbarians had begun to chant.

> *Domnir, Domnir, Blue-Scaled Domnir!*
> *You teach my hands to war, my soul to rage!*
> *None can stand against your flame!*
> *Domnir, Domnir, Blue-Scaled Domnir!*

The blue, serpentine tattoos made a bit more sense, now, but

Masimo Vorenus did not care. Huric the Giant was screaming like a beast, now; he was Rage incarnate, and charged the quickly-thinning legion without regard for his own safety.

Again, Masimo called up the forces of Wind and flew further back. The ground had grown cluttered with bodies. The sun had drawn up a miasma of smells, and vultures circled overhead, ready for their coming feast.

In ten seconds, Huric clove, smashed and gored five more legionaries. Two more arrows struck the berserker, striking the shoulder and stomach; he did not flinch, nor did he stop his charge. Further into the front lines he charged like a bull, splitting a legionary's skull and decapitating another. Masimo flew further back.

I am a coward, he thought. *But at least, I will survive.*

Another spear pierced Huric, this time in the throat, but the bare-chested, white-necked barbarian kept running and swinging. He clove through three more. His entire body dripped with blood—his own, and the legion's. Another spear bit into his chest, into his heart; a javelin flew through and impaled him. Still, he kept swinging.

Maybe he is a god, Masimo wondered, but quickly discounted the thought. Instead, he flew further back.

The impaled, wound-covered Huric killed three more men before a brave legionary charged forward, leapt into the air, and slashed his sword clean through the berserker's neck. Huric's head hit the ground. And his body kept fighting.

He is a god, Masimo thought. *No, he is a demon.*

Huric's headless body killed two more legionaries before another brave legionary knocked him over. A storm of spears punctured the body until he looked like a sponge.

Then a horn blew. Ahead, across the field of bloody, twitching bodies, the barbarian host was charging them, still thousands strong.

The legionaries scattered. Masimo Vorenus called up the power of Wind, and half-ran, half-flew as quickly as possible toward Imperial City.

1049

CHAPTER ONE:
LAST WORDS

Valerio Lucullus, Emperor-Presumptive

The emperor Claudio lay on his deathbed, as calm and stern at the end of his life as he had been in its prime. So much had happened in his reign: wars in the south; raids from the northern barbarians beyond the Wall; and famines and plagues without number. But Emperor Claudio-Valens, the unconquered son of Lucento, worshiped as a living god among his devotees in Eloesus and Haroon, had spared the common citizens from most of the trouble. Throughout his life he had fought at the vanguard, in battle and in life, in war and in discourse. He had not always been popular, but he had always ruled well; and Valerio Lucullus, veteran legate and adoptive "son," feared he could not match his predecessor. He feared that the Golden Age would end.

"Write," said the elderly Claudio-Valens. "I have last words; guidance for your reign."

Valerio nodded. "Yes, my lord emperor."

Valerio transcribed Claudio's words:

Dear Valerio:

In your reign, your goal should be peace. In peacetime, the citizens live long and happy lives. But do not confuse peace with passivity; for peace cannot be achieved except by strength, and by assertion of the Empire's might. Wolves abound in this world, leading the less civilized nations, and they must be deterred, defeated, and humiliated again and again. Nothing attracts these wolves like weakness does; and nothing aids them as much as sedition from within.

Therefore, Valerio Lucullus, veteran of many wars and dear friend, remember these words throughout your rule: Serve your people and your country, and lead at the vanguard like you always have. And, Valerio Lucullus, emperor of this great nation, let your goal therefore always be Conquest; and let your name be Empire.

Valerio set the pen down. He gazed at the former emperor, as his breaths even now grew strained and labored. What a man. What a ruler. What a long, a good and a thoroughly Imperial life.

"And now," Claudio said weakly, "I shall tell you the truth. Do not write this down."

Valerio looked at him uncertainly.

"The world is full of wolves and vipers. Trust no one, Valerio. To survive to my age, you must judge men's character well. Fear your enemies, yes. But fear your friends even more. Trust no one, and when someone gives you reason to mistrust them, get rid of them in whatever capacity they require… send them far away and make them magistrate of some far-flung city, or—if they are truly snakes—find reason to kill them."

Valerio never heard his liege speak like this before. It seemed a bit cynical. Valerio did not mistrust mankind that much; the emperor had become a jaded man indeed. "I will take it to heart," he said.

And there was a knock on the door.

"Come in!" Valerio shouted.

The door opened to reveal Ferro, Marshal of the Imperial Guard. His normally stern, self-assured face was creased with worry, and pale. His pale blue eyes had the shallow look of fear. "An augur has come, Signor Lucullus. The barbarians massacred the legion. They are headed for Imperial City, burning the whole way."

Valerio nodded. *I thought I put the military life behind me.* But he hadn't.

"Your reign faces its first test." The voice of the dying

emperor held the same stern command it did in his youth. "Gods be with you, Valerio."

"And with you as well," he answered. He wondered if this was the last time he'd see Claudio alive.

CHAPTER TWO:
THORNS

Empress Anthea Adamantus

In her private shrine, Anthea clasped the silver statuette of Amara the Mother. She said a prayer to the goddess of motherhood, of friendship and of the love between man and wife. "Please," she whispered, "please do not take my husband from me. He is the last one I trust, the last one I love. My children are far-off, and the palace is a nest of vipers. Please, Lady Love, let me die first… keep my beloved alive." She set the figurine back on the table.

The door behind her was open, and she had already felt a presence there.

"You poor thing." The voice of Melorra, the goddess' own priestess, reassured her. "You cannot change Fate. It is your husband's time to go on to Heaven. In time you will join him. Do not be impatient, my beloved. Besides, you can trust me, can't you?"

Slowly, Anthea rose. Her old bones flared in pain as she turned. "Can I trust you, you say."

Melorra's hairless face was kind indeed. Her blue eyes held such warmth, such compassion. She was Amara in the flesh, a shade of the Mother Goddess.

"No, I cannot trust you." The words weighed heavy on Anthea's heart. "I cannot trust anyone, not even myself."

Melorra frowned.

~

A few palace slaves came to tell her that Claudio neared death. Anthea walked to his bedchamber on her old, weak legs. At the sight of him, tears formed in her eyes. He had rescued her from filth and brought her into greatness. Once, Anthea had been the lowest of all creatures, a whore from the west side slums. Now she was empress, wife Claudio the God; and soon he would be gone from her forever, or at least until she joined him in death. It almost angered her; it almost felt like he insulted her by dying, now.

Are these tears of sadness, she wondered, *or rage?*

"Claudio," she said, and sat on his bed. A hot tear streaked her cheek as she touched his wrinkled face. Once his white hair had been a thick, virile brown. "I love you…" What else was there to say?

"I love you too, Sofia…"

She rose from the bed and walked toward the door. The words struck her like a knife.

"Anthea!" he said, "Anthea!" but the damage was done.

~

Again, she knelt in the shrine, clutching the figurine, but this time she was crying. Again, Melorra was behind her.

"Out of the mouth of the dying come mad things."

She didn't have the strength to respond. She had told Claudio that she forgave him, but how could she? Decades ago, Claudio toured the empire he ruled. Sofia, young daughter of an Eloesian blueblood family, made no secret of Claudio's dalliances there. She had boasted of their affair, proclaimed it so fervently that eventually it reached Anthea's ears half a world away; it had filled her with shame and anger, poisoned her against her husband. She told him she had forgiven him, but had she?

The girl Sofia was dead. Anthea had no part in it, though many suspected her. No, Sofia had died without the empress's involvement. But now, on his deathbed Claudio had said her name. And Anthea could not forgive him, now. She wept, stroking the silver figurine, and prayed for Amara to protect her. She had no one, now; she was alone in this world, a ship cast adrift in a dangerous sea, and the last word of her husband was the name of the girl he had loved. The girl he loved more than her…

"My dear," Melorra said, "your husband loved you."

"Quiet!" Anthea half-wept, half-hissed.

"These grudges, these unplucked thorns, will destroy you if you let them."

"These thorns… they are precious to me." She buckled in, falling to the floor.

A voice shouted from outside her chamber: "The emperor is dead! The emperor is dead! Gods save us all, the emperor is dead!"

CHAPTER THREE:
A RISKY VENTURE

Marcellus Karo

A storm of bells rang over the whole city, even in the Suburro, and that meant only one thing: Claudio-Valens, the emperor, had finally died. But here in the west side, the slovenly citizens cared less about that and more about when the noise would stop. That, of course, and the upcoming match between Theon No-Name and Helmur Bloodaxe; and a thousand other things the bluebloods of the Imperial Palace cared nothing about. Like hunger.

Oh, yes. Hunger. A single loaf of bread—which in the worst times cost a measly copper aes—now cost a whole silver denar. The crop yield in Khazidea had been monstrously low, and the Maestro of Food and Wine had canceled the program of free bread. Now, only the well-to-do could afford to eat. The poor sat on the sides of the streets, and now—months into the famine—their ribs had begun to show and many had collapsed in exhaustion, unable to work. Given that, it was easy to see why no one cared that the emperor died.

Marcellus was hungry, too. The last meal he ate was yesterday afternoon at a dim-lit tavern, a light supper of bread and fish sauce— what the west siders, nowadays, would consider a royal feast—while a certain Bruno Seánus discussed "business" with him. For a price of ten gold sovereigns, Bruno wanted some assistance with the upcoming election… following the death of Marco Petronus, his council seat for Kings Terrace had been vacated. Now, the only two real contenders were Bruno Seánus, and another… Julio Lornodoris, who—though ahead of Bruno in popularity—did not deserve the position, as was made abundantly clear.

It was afternoon, and the gates to Kings Terrace closed at dusk. Otherwise, shady people would enter, rob the mansions and sprawling townhomes of the wealthy August families. Criminals would run through the paved, immaculate streets. Criminals like Marcellus, the assassin and the best of his trade.

~

The gates of Kings Terrace lay open, but a trio of guards in full armor, horsehair-crested helmets and spears stood watch. In name, anyone could pass into Kings Terrace, though the reality was far different. *All citizens are equal, people say, but some are more equal than others.*

Marcellus bit his lip. Even in the fine purple cloak that Bruno Seánus had provided, he couldn't help but worry. He had concealed his dagger perfectly, but he didn't have the full trappings of an August. For one, he didn't talk like them, nor did he have the stern aquiline nose of a Peregothian. His grown hair had an unfortunately light tint, proving his identity as a non-Imperial, an Other, a man of Bregantium.

He was mere yards from the gate when he paused. If something went wrong at the gate, it could compromise his mission. The guards would remember him if he made a fuss. Marcellus knew the city inside and out, better than anyone else. There was another way… a way that few knew besides him. He turned and vanished into an alley.

~

Through the sewers, Marcellus made his way through the dank darkness, the dried sludge and the hideous smells. Careful not to soil his cloak, he followed the route that he knew by heart, through the twisting tunnels in near-total darkness. Ratlings sometimes traveled down here—in fact, it was a ratling friend that showed him—but Marcellus had no worries about them. They kept to themselves, and what they saw in the "undertown" they didn't talk about.

It was too long, marching through the choking stench, but eventually he reached the ladder. When he finally climbed up into the dark, half-burned shack in the shade of a mansion, the outside air smelled like flowers in spring. But here he was, in Kings Terrace, and he hadn't soiled his purple cloak. Now he had to do his work, make certain the right man became Councilor, and collect enough money to live the next few years worry-free.

It always sounded so much easier than it was… both the practical reasons and the emotional ones. After his first kill, he swore he would never do it again. Now, a dozen kills later, it grew easier but it still wasn't easy. Unlike most Black Serpent assassins, Marcellus had the weakness of a heart.

~

Once on the street, he felt more at ease; no one looked at him with suspicion or turned their heads when he walked by. After all, the streets were mostly empty, save a few guards… in the distance, a grand dame in a billowing blue dress and her gaggle of handmaidens turned down some thoroughfare. A pair of blueblood men in purple tunics walked by, perhaps talking business, and paid Marcellus no heed. He felt unworried, but guarded against pride; it had been the undoing of so many Black Serpents before him.

Quiet and composed, he made his way through Kings Terrace. The sprawling mansions of the Augusts often took up entire blocks. But even the more modest townhomes—thanks to their location— were expensive beyond a west sider's greatest imaginings. How often did Marcellus hear that all were equal in the eyes of the emperor, and how eagerly did he believe it. The Augusts of Kings Terrace lived in a different world, a place far-removed from the slums of the west side.

He shrugged off the creeping sense of envy; it would only cloud his judgment. Through the clean paved streets, beside the green gardens, he walked, until at last, he reached the Lornodoris home.

Even in Kings Terrace, it was in a class of its own. Twice the size of the largest mansion Marcellus had seen, it dominated two city blocks and rose three stories into the air. An iron-grilled gate blocked all entry. Four guards stood watch there, wearing mixed plate and mail armor with purple capes and helmets with purple horsehair crests.

The Lornodoris family had once been greater, but sometime after Claudio-Valens became emperor their political clout waned. It was a blueblood concern of the Augusts, and Marcellus wouldn't give it any thought. He had one mission: to make certain that Julio Lornodoris died, overcome all guilt, and leave no trace—either to him, or to his client, as the Black Serpent code demanded.

~

He tried a dozen ways to get in the alley behind the Lornodoris home. At last, sometime in late afternoon after circumventing several mansions and climbing over a roof, he managed to drop into the alley, and wait. He crouched there in the shade and took out the clump of blackcrystal—his poison of choice because, if dissolved in water, it caused severe heart trouble several hours after the fact. There'd be no way to tell for certain if Julio had died of poison, and only Marcellus would know.

He sat there silently, and waited.

~

At twilight, Marcellus prepared to make his entry. He pocketed the blackcrystal again. High above, an iron-grilled window led inside. Enough to deter any common bandit, but Marcellus was a Black Serpent, and he had a way in.

More specifically, something to cut the grill. He took out the sharp-edged, bluish file. The secret was *adamant*, the latest invention of the Alchemist Collegium, a metal stronger than steel that took its name from the late emperor. Expensive beyond even most Augusts' means, the only reason Marcellus had one was thanks to the Black Serpent Majordomo and his connections.

Up Marcellus climbed, finding footholds where no one else would. His friends called him Marcellus the Spider. He peeked through the window through the grill, and saw an empty bedroom.

At once he began to work the file, sawing through the iron bars. The process lasted a few minutes, but eventually, the iron bars fell, one-by-one. He tried the window, pulling hard against the wooden panel. His deft fingers had taught him to open windows of all difficulties, and—eventually—with a shudder, the window gave way. He pushed it the rest of the way and slipped in.

The Lornodoris home smelled of spices and simmering cookpots. Marcellus' stomach growled in response. Out in the streets of Suburro and the west side, people wasted away to skeletons, but here, a royal feast was underway.

The walls of the bedchamber were painted with waves, fish, and seahorse-drawn chariots. Unsurprising, since the Lornodorsi worshiped Lorenus the sea god as their patron. Toys scattered on the floor—dolls, blocks, and miniature soldiers—not to mention the small bed, proved that whoever slept in this room was not Marcellus' target.

~

He stalked through the winding halls of the Lornodoris mansion, watching out for movement. He followed the strengthening scent of spice and searing meat. At last, through a narrow corridor, he heard the chattering of slaves and the *clink* of cookpots and utensils.

He felt a draft behind him. A deep voice spoke: "Who are you? What are you doing here?"

Marcellus whipped around; his right hand went to his dagger, the other two his swab of basilisk poison. He was already moving, his blade was already swathed, when he looked at his foe: a man in a chain shirt and a pointed blue-plumed helmet. He was drawing his sword when Marcellus hammered the dagger through an opening in the neck. A second later, the guard hit the floor trembling. Within a minute the poison would kill him.

Marcellus panted, looking at his handiwork as a cold sweat trickled over every inch of him. *I've made a mistake,* he thought. *One that I should have avoided.* It was necessary to kill him because of Marcellus' own carelessness, but it was sloppy. Any hope of concealing the murder was gone; poisoning the wineglass would only make things needlessly complicated.

He stalked ahead. The clatter of the cookpots only added to Marcellus' growing restlessness. He had killed a guard, and chaos would overtake the household as soon as he was found. *Better that the guard isn't found,* he thought at first. Then he determined to execute his plan as quickly as possible, and vanish into the night.

He peeked down the other end of the hallway. A guard with a similar pointed feather-plumed iron cap stood there. *Perhaps they knew each other. They will meet soon in Hell.*

Ducking against the wall, Marcellus soaked another swab with basilisk venom, then wiped it on the dagger. He charged, and within two seconds' time the dagger-blade was inside the guard's neck, and his other hand covered the mouth. He slumped to the ground and at last collapsed.

But chaos was breaking loose in the feasting hall. The family, dining on a first course of bread and grapes, had erupted into shouting. The head of the Lornodoris family—sitting on a raised dais with his much-too-young wife—was shouting obscenities, red-faced. As Marcellus sprang table-to-table like they were stones in a river, the young blonde wife of Julio fled her massive husband, who could not move by himself. In his cherry-knuckled, gouty hands he clutched a half-eaten chicken leg like a weapon.

A slash to the throat and Julio began gargling. Two more strikes, one toward the heart, another across the chest. *What a monster I've become.*

A hand from behind jerked the hood off him. He turned around and saw the culprit: a swarthy Eloesian slave. In the distance, a child's voice: "Father?"

While the other feasters had fled the scene, a wide-eyed, blond little boy stood in the doorway. As Marcellus sawed through the screaming Eloesian's neck, he knew he would have to kill everyone who had seen his face. But looking in the innocent little Lornodoris' eyes, he wondered—even after the hundreds he had killed—whether he had the ability.

CHAPTER FOUR:
THE ARRIVAL

Anthea Adamantus

In the Yellow Chair, a barely-composed Anthea Adamantus viewed the Imperial Council's impassioned discussion.

"The funeral is tomorrow," said the Speaker of the Council, Edesso Vitellus, "so long as Lucento arrives by tonight."

Her son, Lucento-Valens—named after Claudio's father—and his wife Lysandra had not been to Imperial City in years. It would be good to see them at last. Sometimes Anthea wondered if the East had changed her son, corrupted him perhaps; the people there viewed his father as a god, and perhaps him as well. At the thought, she despaired.

"There has been rioting in the streets," Edesso said. "The people are hungry. One man killed a guard; they cut him up and left him in Imperial Square for all to see."

"Lay into them with force. We can't tolerate that kind of behavior!" growled Councilor Donello, a firebrand from Nichaeus. "Once enough of them die, they will stop rioting."

"No!" Anthea snapped. They all turned their heads; it was so rare for her to speak during these meetings. "The people are hungry. We are so used to our luxurious lives, we don't understand. *None* of you understand. The famine in Khazidea is to blame, not them. I will not have you kill any of them. They are rioting because they have no other recourse."

Edesso kept staring at her for a few more minutes, then nodded. "Yes, Your Worship." He cleared his throat and looked over the next item on the lectern.

When Anthea scanned the circular room, she couldn't help but notice Amaraeus. The slave, of uncertain origin, had been Claudio's favorite. Now, he served as Maestro of the Treasury. He had whittled all the unnecessary expenses of the Imperial Palace, and now a surplus of money flowed into the coffers every year. Still, there were things she could not overcome. He had concealed Claudio's affair with Sofia, though he had been in his retinue when it happened. He had spoken ill of Anthea to him, called her proud and guileful, unaccepting of her place as a docile wife. But those were only small things; more than that, she saw in Amaraeus' golden eyes a cunning ambition, a desire to rise to the top at the expense of anyone—including, and perhaps most of all, Anthea.

The Maestro of the Treasury had the coppery skin of a Khazidee, but the color had a browner, earthier tone, and his face—though handsome—had features Anthea had never seen before. When she tried to inquire of his origins, the Maestro of the Treasury refused to discuss it; more fuel for her suspicions.

"A massacre in Kings Terrace," Edesso began. "A savage assault on the Lornodoris home. Blood everywhere. Forty people stabbed to death; somehow the assassin prevented anyone from escaping."

Anthea paled. The news reminded her of how, in this world, no one was safe.

"Julio Lornodoris' throat was cut," Edesso continued. "The Commander of the City Watch says that Julio's son was left alive... he is being questioned as we speak."

"Wasn't he after Councilor Petronus' seat?" asked Councilor Durantus.

"Yes," Edesso said grimly. "Thanks to his untimely demise, it's near certain that Bruno Seánus will win the election."

"Do you think it's possible that Bruno—" Donello's voice trailed off.

"Don't be absurd," Edesso snarled.

Indeed, the thought was too wicked to contemplate, even for Anthea. Bruno had always been kind to her; he was incapable of such evil.

"Some think that the death cult of Balzor is responsible."

Some blame everything on the worshipers of the death god. Still, they did exist, meeting in catacombs or cemeteries or the "spice gardens" of the west side.

"Regardless, the perpetrator will be sentenced to death by burning." Edesso looked down and moved on to the next item.

Surely the murder of an entire family deserves more time.

"The provincials are getting restless. The emperor has not toured the nation for many years, and some think that Imperial City has forgotten about them."

"As soon as we have finished the business of the funeral," Anthea said, "I will send Valerio. We can appoint a regent to rule in his absence."

For some reason, Anthea's gaze had wandered back to Amaraeus and his golden, scheming eyes. At the thought, she went cold. A slave could not be regent, she remembered and exhaled.

An attendant hurried through the meeting room's open doors. "Good councilors, Lucento and Lady Lysandra have arrived in the harbor."

For the first time in several hours, Anthea stood up. The council's bickering could wait. It was time to meet her son.

~

Lucento did not have Claudio's dark, virile hair, nor his commanding presence (though he did have some) but he had his father's blood. She could see that in how the palace slaves bowed before him and tended to his every whim.

But when her auburn-haired, blue-eyed son looked into her eyes, she smiled. As she embraced him, she thought of what she had seen. He did seem changed, weary perhaps. And his eyes seemed different, darker maybe, or just harsher. Still, her eyes watered. "My dear son. It is so good to see you."

"Mother," Lucento said, "I feel just the same."

When she backed away, she realized what was different about his eyes. They looked different, more violet than blue. *Has he been using spice?* The thought unnerved her.

When Lysandra, the Eloesian grand dame, walked in, the reception was slightly colder. "Lady Anthea." She curtsied. Her eyes, once blue, had gone almost completely red.

Spice indeed. What has become of my family?

Lady Lysandra's azure gown was interwoven with silk thread and studded with diamonds and chalcedony. Two slaves held up the train. Her coiffed blonde hair was held up high, complementing her white-powdered face perfectly. She was everything Anthea hadn't been at her age: an Eloesian aristocrat, a wealthy heiress, a blueblood to the innermost sinew. *So why does she use Haroon spice?*

Her children followed after her: a boy of about seven, dressed in a purple, diamond-studded tunic, who had his grandfather's dark brown hair. Two girls, one blonde and one dark, one three and one five, followed behind him in miniature dresses just as elaborate as their mother's. Born into the purple, and fed by a silver spoon. *They know nothing of life.*

"It is good to see you, Lysandra," Anthea said.

Lysandra nodded.

Not even a word to spare. Though she had co-ruled the empire, even her family treated her coldly.

~

She was heading to her bedchamber, ready to confide once again in Melorra and the mother goddess, when a piercing trumpet resounded. For a second, she went cold, thinking that perhaps the barbarians had overcome Emperor Valerio and routed his troops; but the trumpet pealed again, and she knew it was Imperial.

When Valerio and a dozen Imperial Guards made their way into the palace, they had brought a visitor. The odorous creature they had brought into the grand hall was a barbarian—that much was clear—and fleas swarmed about his blood-soiled jerkin. He smelled of a thousand different things, death being chief among them. His greasy, unshorn blond hair was so repulsive to Anthea that she nearly gagged.

"This smelly thing calls himself Lothar. He says he is a king. Tell him yourself." Valerio half-grinned—a strange sight, since Valerio had never smiled nor shown any sort of emotion before.

Lothar's ice-blue eyes regarded Anthea. He spoke the Imperial tongue in a harsh accent that removed all its beauty: "I am Lothar, the war chief."

His breath was even fouler than his clothing.

"Why did you attack our country?" Valerio asked.

"You southlanders have everything… our winters grow colder each year. The crops produce less and less. The Blue Dragon urges us to war and we will not refuse his call. You southlanders have forgotten how to struggle and how to fight. You have lost your courage. You have lost the strength that built the Empire. Your people are cowards. The king of Bregantium—"

Governor.

"—emptied the treasury without a fight. Sloth has weakened you—"

"Enough!" Anthea snapped. "I won't hear him anymore."

"He'll be executed at sundown."

"No." Anthea bit her trembling lip. "Perhaps we should let him go."

Valerio hesitated.

In the distance, Lysandra stormed over. "Let him go?" She laughed poisonously. "I have heard that your late husband conquered Khazidea single-handedly. I hoped some of his courage rubbed off on you. How wrong I was."

"Quiet!" Anthea managed not to call her *lupa.* "Do what you will, Valerio. I'm not sure what purpose his death will serve." She walked away, toward the couch where her son Lucento sat, and Valerio's wife, the empress Issadore.

She is empress now. I am empress no longer. The realization made her eyes water, but life would have to go on.

CHAPTER FIVE:
SECRETS

Melorra, Beloved of the Mother

Melorra had pledged her soul in a bond of love to Anthea—not the love of man and wife, but the love of a sister to a sister as children of the heavenly Mother of all. That was why she searched through the guest's belongings, careful to leave everything as it was: to guard her beloved against the poison vipers of this world, the selfish and cruel god-haters that lurked in every corner.

With her shepherd's crook, she lifted up one of Lysandra's dresses, seeing nothing underneath it as she expected. The wooden chests of luggage may prove more ominous, she thought. She crossed the room and unlatched one; a cloth covered it, and she removed a corner. Underneath were piles of spice packets. She paled, remembering the crimson eyes of Lysandra, and scolded herself for not knowing. Among the spice packets, she also found a fetish of a black snake twined around a tree.

She shuddered. The good son and daughter-in-law of Anthea Adamantus, worshiping the Black Serpent? Her sisters in Eloesus had told of the evil cult, originating in the south and brought to the Empire: of the spice-fueled debauches, of the sacrifices of Eloesian lowbloods, of the snake-handlers who claimed immunity to cobra venom, and of the murderers who killed in the Serpent's name. It was a cult of the Eloesian aristocracy that preyed on the poor and the homeless, the lost souls that Melorra and her sisters were supposed to protect.

Still, it was not something she would hurry back and tell her lady about. Wicked as it was, she would inform her after the funeral, after she had recovered from her departed husband's loss. She fingered through the spice packets, reached the wooden bottom, and realized no other secrets hid within this chest.

Another chest had dried emergency provisions. Yet another

contained Lady Lysandra's cosmetics. Then another, positioned in the corner, beckoned to her. She hesitated, wondering if she served Lady Anthea in the way that she wanted. But she bit her lip, overcame her inhibition, and walked over, unclasping the iron hinges.

After a cloth layer, a pile of papers met Melorra's eyes. The first few were of no consequence—letters to this person or that in Imperial City—but beneath was a velvet coinpurse, heavy with gold, and a letter addressed to a man named "Qabo Eightfingers, majordomo in the Black Serpent's absence."

She read on:

To the Lair in Imperial City: a certificate of payment, to the amount of ten gold sovereigns, for your good work in Eloesus, hand delivered in the year 1049 by the Lady Lysandra. A heartfelt thanks on behalf of her entire household.

Before she could read any further, a voice sent her sprawling to her feet. "In Imperial City, are spies tolerated?"

She whipped around. An Eloesian guard in halfplate stood in the doorway with a spear. A cold sweat swept over her. She withered under the man's gaze. Panic overtook all conscious thought; her heart raced out of control. *Give me clarity of thought and wisdom, Mother.*

"In Korthos, do you know what we do with sneaks? We remove their troublesome eyes, so that they cannot lurk about again. Now come with me, what is your name—"

"Melorra."

"Melorra, I will escort you to the dungeon. The warden may be half-mad, but Lysandra Adamantus will certainly hold more sway over him than a bald, homely witch."

Despair crept over her as she realized he spoke truth. The warden had no love of Melorra or her mother goddess. Melorra had spoken too many times against his tortures, his cruel treatment of prisoners in the ill-lit, ill cared-for dungeon.

As the guard walked toward her, Melorra cried out: "Please, let me speak with my lady Anthea first. Please, please. The empress Anthea—"

"She isn't empress any longer, my dear." The guard gave her an evil grin, the grin of someone who knew nothing of the Mother's compassion or lovingkindness. "Lady Lysandra will see you tonight, once everyone is in bed. She is a fine lady, and beautiful, but she does not deal well with spies or sneaks. May the gods save you when you face her fury."

When the guard's hand gripped her arm, she nearly fell limp. *Ah! May the goddess save me indeed.* She tried not to whimper as the guard half-led, half-dragged her out of the room.

CHAPTER SIX:
THE FUNERAL

Anthea Adamantus

The limestone jar was all that was left of him. His ashes would lie in the Temple of Imperium until the end of the world or the end of the Empire, whichever came first. Anthea didn't think her late husband had any regrets. He had succeeded in every endeavor he set his mind upon. He had overcome so many challenges and brought the world to its knees. The Easterners worshipped him as a god. And now he was dust.

King and pauper, man and woman, slave and free—all become dust in the end. Melorra had read the verse from the Book of Love.

Where is Melorra? As the Pontifex, in his gem-studded miter, droned on and on, she looked around. There was Lady Lysandra in her white brocade dress… Anthea's son Lucento in his fine purple tunic and his children in their small clothes… Valerio and Issadore Lucullus. Her gaze met Amaraeus' golden eyes, and she took in a sudden gasp.

Melorra would not miss the funeral for the world, nor abandon her for anything—not even her own life. Something prevented her. Either that, or something happened to her. She gasped again. She would not survive the palace's treachery without her. Melorra was her one hope, her one friend.

Trumpets blared and Anthea stumbled forward. Ferro, Marshal of the Guard, and a dozen of his men walked from a side door. In Ferro's callused hands was the will. Once in front of the limestone urn, he broke the seal and began to read:

"Here is the will of the great emperor Claudio the Divine, sovereign of the six nations and shepherd of the people, who has ruled always with a just and unrelenting hand: I put the Empire in the capable hands of Valerio Lucullus, who has proven himself a warrior and a great leader of men. I pardon Marowyn the halfling princess that rebelled against our benevolent rule, and command Valerio not to punish Kalamar in any way. I pardon also her accomplice husband Darosha. I send my eternal love to my lady wife—"

Anthea bit her lip so as not to smile, but tears began to form.

"—and command that the Maestro of the Treasury send her whatever money she requires. I free Aleria Lycurga. I free Septimo Boreus. I free Amaraeus No-Name, appoint him Maestro of Justice, and appoint Tribo Tertius as Maestro of the Treasury in his stead."

Anthea wanted to faint right then and there, but she couldn't show weakness at a time like this. Now, as a freed slave, Amaraeus was a part of the household he had belonged to… the Imperial household. The ambitious demon would do whatever it took to climb to the top. He was ruthless and Claudio never understood. Claudio never realized what fire he was playing with, but Anthea knew.

A tear streaked her cheek despite her best efforts. She needed Melorra at times like this. She needed her kind eyes, her love, and her mother goddess. *Where is Melorra? Goddess, where is Melorra?*

Amaraeus was glowing now. A smile spread from one giant ear to the other.

A demon has been loosed into the world.

At the small gathering in the feasting hall, Anthea didn't touch the pork-stuffed dormice. Instead, she sipped at her hippocras absently. The people around her talked among themselves, ignoring her. Even her son ignored her.

My own son.

"I will be touring the Empire starting tomorrow," Emperor Valerio told Councilor Edesso. "When Claudio toured, it took a year, didn't it?"

"Yes. And he was younger than you, then. It's best to pace yourself." Edesso laughed. "You wouldn't want Issadore to tire and take ill, would you?"

"She is not coming," Valerio said. "I begged her but she's

been having terrible headaches in the past few days. I worry for her."

"Ah, she'll wait for you eagerly I'm sure. I've never seen a woman more smitten with her husband."

I am alone in this world. They are ignoring me, and I am alone. She rose. Nobody noticed. She left the feasting hall toward the women's apartments.

~

She clutched the silver figurine of Amara. She prayed in tears.

"My mother, my goddess, I place everything under your loving care. I am at an end. The palace is full of vipers. I don't know where your servant is gone. Please, don't take Melorra from me. I cannot live without her."

Where could she be?

CHAPTER SEVEN:
CRUELTY

Melorra, Beloved of the Mother

Two cords wrapped around her wrists, two more around her ankles. She was suspended in the middle of the room, completely naked and bleeding all over. The Eloesian bodyguard, Leonas, was a cruel man for certain, but he was not the worst.

No. When Lysandra's white-powdered face appeared in the dim dungeon light, Melorra knew the true tormentress had arrived. She would have cried out, but she was out of breath. In her hand she held the whip Melorra had learned to fear.

"I want the truth, *lupa*," the Eloesian dame hissed. "I want the truth, and then I will end your pain. Leonas will put his dagger through your throat and I won't have to hear your wicked voice. So answer me, *lupa*, what did you see?"

"Nothing!" *What is such a small lie to the Mother of all?*

The whip cut into her and her body bristled with pain. It hurt as badly as she remembered; she'd never get used to it. Tears formed in her eyes and dripped down. She began to sob.

She called out, "Mother preserve us!" She prayed, *Amara, guide my beloved unto me.*

"The Black Snake will eat your Mother and spit out her mangled flesh," Lysandra hissed. Leonas chuckled at her words.

Another lashing, and Melorra wondered if it would be best to leave this loveless world. Then she remembered Anthea her beloved, and determined to remain alive for her sake.

Amara, guide my beloved unto me.

A lash answered her prayer.

CHAPTER EIGHT:
BLACK SERPENT

Marcellus Karo

Go into the "wine cellar" of Benetto's Tavern in the Suburro, open the secret door, and a world opens up to you. Even though he was one of them, every time Marcellus entered the Black Serpent Lair he felt unwelcome and perhaps in danger. The red walls, lit with flickering oil lamps, had a black snake figure running from one end of the massive complex to the other.

Immediately greeting him was a couch stained with the bile of overwhelmed spice users, trickles of blood, and worse things. Regardless of the filth, Claretta—the Black Serpent strumpet—lay lengthwise across it in her short black skirt and midriff, and she greeted Marcellus with a "Hail!" and lust-glazed eyes.

"Claretta." Marcellus smiled. Whatever dalliances with her would have to wait. The majordomo had summoned him, but even then, looking at Claretta's perfect form and dark eyes, he couldn't deny that his body was responding in kind. "I have business with the majordomo."

He walked past her, into the network of equally-red corridors and rooms, filled with poison vials and assassins' tools and weaponry racks. But at last he reached the Black Door, knocked three times, and waited.

Seconds later, a voice answered: "Come in."

Qabo did not look pleased. The swarthy, scar-faced man never looked pleased, but he looked less pleased than usual. The sightless eye, injured—he said—in a battle of the Desolation, seemed to be no hindrance to his trade. Qabo Eightfingers was the best assassin in the Empire and probably the world. He had turned killing into an art form.

He had made the Magistrate of Eximenius' death look like a suicide. He had framed the Magistrate of Hieronea for a legate's death, and made an Imperial ambassador's demise look like an accidental drowning. And most importantly, he had gotten away with it. If you needed someone dead, and you knew the right people, there was only one person to ask.

The legendary assassin did not look pleased to see him. "That was the worst job I've ever seen," Qabo said. "Even for you, Marcellus, it was terrible. An entire household massacred. A bloody mess. There's no art to that. No skill. You are a disappointment. And worst of all, you left that boy alive."

Marcellus flushed in shame. "Yes, signore. My compassion got the best of me."

"Compassion." It was an almost an exhale. "You are pathetic. The whole City Watch is after you. I would say you're on your own. But if they caught you, I know your compassion would make you tell everything about us."

He knew where this was headed.

"You've gone soft, Marcellus. You know what happens when Black Serpents go soft?"

Qabo's four-fingered hand suddenly had a dagger in it, but Marcellus' blow was already coming. The blade stuck him in the shoulder. Marcellus ducked Qabo's blow and ran.

At the door Claretta gasped; Marcellus kicked it open and felt something sharp stick him in the back, stealing his breath. *A throwing knife.* More assassins were coming. Marcellus flew through the door, clambering up the stairs even as he bled.

Upstairs, a half-clothed woman performed an exotic southron dance before her admirers. Benetto—behind the bar—started screaming: "What is the meaning of this? What are you doing? Get out of here, street-trash."

He barreled forward, running through the filthy streets of the

Suburro. A woman hurled a chamber pot from high above and the ungodly stink splashed over him.

"Balzor take you!" Marcellus screamed as the stench flooded over him. He kept running. He jerked his head to look behind him. A four-fingered hand was reaching for his cloak. Another four-fingered hand held a dagger dripping blue, and a one-eyed face snarled at him.

His legs were giving out. The throwing knife had been dipped in something and who knew what? If it were basilisk poison, he'd be dead already.

But he was stumbling. His legs gave in and he felt hard, cracking his cheekbones against the street. Qabo's dagger did not pierce him. When he rolled over, he saw why: an armored man wearing a war-eagle surcoat, examining him closely. A city watchman. They had caught the rat.

CHAPTER NINE: MOTHER'S MERCY

Melorra, Beloved of the Mother

"What is the meaning of this?"

Anthea's incredulous screech was like the Mother's own voice.

Melorra was dripping all over the floor. A pool of blood had nearly dried down from where she hung, suspended. "My beloved, shield your eyes. A woman like you should never see such suffering."

"I won't shield my eyes, Melorra. What in Varda is going on?"

"My beloved, Lady Lysandra has lost her way. She has done this to me; and how can I not pity a woman of such a hard heart?"

"Pity?" Melorra's words seemed to anger Anthea more than the injustice itself; she should have chosen different ones. "If you won't stand up for yourself, I'll do it for you. I'll have Lysandra's head."

"Do not answer violence with violence."

"Shut up!" she screamed. She sounded half-mad. "Give your platitudes to a better woman. I can't handle them. I will have you cleaned and pampered until you're back to health. And I *will* have Lysandra's head."

There was no use arguing.

"I thought Leonas served Lysandra."

Melorra smiled as warmly as she could manage. "His heart is not as hard as Lysandra. I convinced him to walk in the Mother's way. I prayed with him to the Three Graces and their Seven Mercies, and now they carry his words to the Mother like sweet incense. So he did tell you I was here. What a wondrous change of heart."

Anthea did not answer. The white-haired matron was simmering; she had that look. Melorra hated that look. But it was wondrous to see her beloved after so many hours or days or weeks in bondage. *Mother, you are merciful. Thank you.*

CHAPTER TEN:
FAMINE'S SICKLE

Anthea Adamantus

Advisors and maestros and doting palace servants swarmed over Anthea as soon as she emerged from the misery of the dungeon, but as soon as she reached the Grand Hall and stood within hearing range, she screamed: "*Arrest Lysandra!*"

By the grace of the Mother, Ferro and a few Imperial Guards were there.

"They left the palace, Your Worship, just moments ago," Ferro said. "They might be at the harbor already."

"Then run! I want her, and I want her now—"

"Why—" The guard stopped himself when Melorra's bleeding form appeared. Anthea put her hand around the poor, trembling thing.

As Ferro and the guards sprinted through the doors in a whirl of red capes, Anthea raised her voice again: "I want a sickbed near my quarters and a physician *at once*."

A dozen palace slaves scattered off to achieve the goals first. Anthea sat down in one of the couches in the Grand Hall.

Long after a slave took Melorra to her sickbed, and long after the palace slaves began scrubbing the blood from the floor, Ferro returned with ten members of the Guard.

"Your Worship," Ferro knelt before her. "I had just reached the harbor when they left. Lysandra is gone."

"Gone," Anthea breathed, and buried her face in her hands. "Mother preserve us! How could my son have fallen in with such a demoness? I have failed my children. My only son…"

"There is Claudian…" Ferro's regretful expression proved he

knew how deep the words wounded her.

"Yes… yes… there is Claudian."

In her private shrine, she clasped the silver figurine of Amara and prayed to the goddess in her Heavenly home. "Oh, sweet Mother, I am not like you. I am not a good mother like you. I am not even good."

Claudian was older than Lucento, maybe forty years of age now. But he could not take care of himself. He hadn't spoken words until age five. Anthea placed him in a monastery in Sanctum. At the time she thought she did what was best for him. She thought… *All this thinking has turned me into a wretch. No wonder people loathe my presence.*

"Your Worship."

Anthea gasped at the low voice. She turned around and met the pallid visage of Lycano Geta, Maestro of Food and Wine. His ice-blue eyes—which she once thought had been impossible to thaw—betrayed his worry.

"We flirt with disaster. There is rioting in Imperial Square, as I told Amaraeus—"

Don't say that name.

"—and a woman, some flea-bitten wench from Mud Bottom, cooked her own child in a pot. There are witnesses…"

"Well, she should die." Anthea stroked her figurine. "Clearly. That is a wicked crime."

"And something Amaraeus is worrying about. He is the Maestro of Justice, after all."

That name. Anthea felt sick.

"People are eating dogs and cats."

Anthea grimaced.

"Others are going through garbage. Simply put, Anthea, the people are starving. We'll be a city of skeletons in no time. I am old enough to remember the famine of 1036—"

And I am old enough to have seen you in swaddling clothes.

"—and Imperial City was well-prepared for it then. We are not prepared, Your Worship. In time, the only people with food will be in the palace."

"You do realize that *you* are the Maestro of Food and Wine. You should have prepared for it."

Lycano glared. "Regardless, Your Worship, something needs to be done."

"Open the palace stockpiles. Feed whoever you can, and wisely. If Famine's sickle slays the citizens, then it will slay the bluebloods as well. We will *all* starve."

"It will not be popular in the p—"

"Popular!" Anthea scoffed. "You know nothing of governing. Popularity should be the least of a ruler's concerns."

"Valerio is the emperor, Your W—"

"*Do it*," Anthea snarled, and Lycano backed away as if driven off by an angry wolf.

Anthea took her bread and wine in private that evening. She could sense the anger already. They could have lasted two years in the palace on the stockpiles. But if the citizens would starve, then so would Anthea and the rest of the bluebloods.

She had not eaten such meager fare in decades. She wept as she nibbled at the plain bread and sipped at the weak, watered-down wine. Sitting in her private chamber, she asked for the Mother's mercy, but even the great goddess would not listen. She never did. She hadn't given life back to Claudio. She had given her a brigand as a son, and a wicked Eastern witch as a daughter-in-law.

Soon after she began the bare meal, it was over. The weak wine sickened her. And Lycanos stood there at her bedroom door. At the sight of his blue eyes, her eyes began to water. His expression was grim.

"We came to distribute the food." Lycanos hesitated, perhaps unsure of whether to continue. "A mob attacked and stole it. It turned into a free-for-all. The city is in chaos now. I am certain there will be blood on the streets tonight. And what will happen to the corpses, I wonder—"

"*Leave me!*" Anthea screamed. "*Leave me, Lycanos!*"

And he did.

CHAPTER ELEVEN:
TABLES TURNED

Marcellus Karo

Marcellus' vision cleared. He lay on a sickbed in a stone room, and two men stood there by him. One—a wizened man in a long green tunic—had a steaming bowl of foul-smelling liquid. *A physician.*

The other had the look of someone very important, or at least someone who considered himself to be. Tall and thin, his skin had a dark brown color and his eyes a light gold. His dark blackish hair, though cut thin, had a thick look to it. Most important of all, his white tunic had a purple sash. This was a man of great import… an Imperial title at the minimum. So why was he here, overseeing the recovery of a criminal from the west side?

"Quite a bloody scene you made," the gold-eyed man said and smiled. "Sloppy, perhaps, but probably not your best work."

"It certainly was not," Marcellus said.

"Little Julio saw you murder his father. He claims you were the culprit. Is it true?"

"Yes. Wait, no." *This poison destroyed my judgment.*

"Careful with your words," the gold-eyed man said. "You want to be kept alive, don't you? You do understand… if you are not the assassin, I will kill you and claim that justice was served—they'll hear it from little Julio, and believe. If you *are* the assassin, you possess a useful talent that may warrant keeping you alive."

"I did it," Marcellus breathed.

The gold-eyed man turned to the physician. "Signore, would you say the poison is healed?"

The physician nodded.

"Ferro!" the gold-eyed man shouted.

The doors opened, and a man in heavy armor and a red halfcloak strode in. His broadsword was unsheathed and in his hand, at the ready. He shut the door behind him.

Marcellus tensed up. *What is going on?*

The gold-eyed man nodded and the man grabbed the physician's shoulder in his gauntlet-lined hand.

"What is the meaning of this?" the physician cried.

Before he could speak again, the man's broadsword was through his throat, and blood dripping down his green tunic like brown veins.

Marcellus gasped. The gold-eyed man turned around and crossed the room. He came back holding an ash-colored monk's habit.

"Remove your clothes. Such bare attire is common among the Monks Militant of the Priesthood of Kharn. That's where you will be headed. The Ironfist Monastery is on the sea, ten days' journey by foot, from the city limits. With enough inquiry you will find the way. Leave along the Path of Tidus. Understood?"

"Yes. Ehrm, signore…" He half-pointed to the physician, still shaking in his death-throes.

"With enough cutting, no one will think twice about his face."

Marcellus' stomach turned at the thought.

"Few physicians matched your body so perfectly. In your clothes there will be no difference. Now strip."

Still in shock, Marcellus stood up and nearly fell over. But in time, he got around to the job at hand.

"You will wait in the Ironfist Monastery until I give you further orders, and you will speak to no one of this, not even Father Catellus. Do not worry. You won't have to take any vows of poverty or chastity—"

"Thank Heavens."

"—and there is one more thing."

Marcellus draped the cloak over himself and raised the hood. The other man, Ferro, offered a handful of silver denara. Weakly, he pocketed the cold metal objects.

"As the Maestro of Justice, I know certain things. For example, we've long suspected that there is a group of murderers-for-hire in the city—"

"Assassins," Marcellus interjected.

"And I would be remiss in my duty if I didn't put an end to that. So, in exchange for your life and your upcoming mission, I demand the location of this murderers' nest."

"The Serpent Lair. Yes, yes." Marcellus turned his eyes from Ferro's ruthless cutting. He sickened as he told this gold-eyed man everything. He had betrayed the Black Serpents and brought on the Lair's certain doom—but perhaps it was for his own good.

CHAPTER TWELVE:
THE DEMON ASCENDANT

Anthea Adamantus

It was still dark when Anthea awoke to screams. She started awake, hauling her fragile old self across the room in a panic, out into the corridor. It was Melorra screaming. By the time Anthea got to the room, she had quieted, but the bald priestess's eyes were wide with fear.

Anthea had never seen Melorra afraid. It unnerved her. "My dear, what is wrong?" She hobbled as fast as she could to the side of the bed.

"I've had a night terror. I don't remember the half of it, but it was such a horrid dream, my beloved. I hope you never have the likes of it."

Anthea clasped Melorra's hand. "We must stick together. We are both sisters under one Mother."

"True." She seemed deeply shaken.

"What was the dream?"

"Fire," Melorra said. "Fire raining from above, and fire bursting from the earth's deepest vents. And a mountain… a terrible red mountain! The earth shuddering beneath our feet like birth pains."

"Do you think there will be an earthquake? Our people can recover from that. Destructive ones are rare, sister."

"Hush." Melorra had never said that to her, before. "I am close to the Mother. I feel her worry and her fear. If the Mother is afraid, then we should all be afraid. And the Mother is certainly not afraid of a mere earthquake."

Anthea almost told her to be quiet, but even now—as her heart raced—she could never speak so disrespectfully to Melorra. "It's just a dream," Anthea said, against her intuition. "There is nothing to worry about, Melorra."

"Anthea." Melorra was covered in cold sweat, and with her dried bloody wounds she looked wretched indeed. "You are a good woman, kind, and strong as adamant, but you are not wiser than me. I know when a dream is simply a dream. And this, my beloved, is more. For our own sakes, we should worry. I still do not know what it means, but I felt the Mother's fear. Be careful in the coming hours, my empress. Watch yourself, though I do not know what you should watch for."

Anthea had gone so cold she felt frozen, unable to speak. Instead, she rose, gathered herself, and walked away.

Again, she took her breakfast—stale bread soaked in broth—in her private chambers. She thanked the gods that Lycano Geta did not show his face. She had just finished when another man arrived—Councilor Galleo Durantus, wearing his purple stripe proudly. "The Council is convening, Your Worship. I thought you should know."

She peered into the man's blue eyes. She sensed worry. *Yes, I will go*, she thought. "I will go."

Anthea sat her old bones down on the Yellow Seat. The White Seat, where the emperor would normally sit, was, as she expected, vacant.

A full twenty-nine councilors sat in the chambers—Bruno Seánus, the newest addition, having the pleased look of a man that achieved a lifelong goal—with Speaker Edesso Vitellus at the lectern. She gazed this way and that, eyeing these old men, many of whom her husband Claudio had forcefully appointed. When her eyes reached a shadowy corner, the gold eyes reflecting back unraveled her.

Amaraeus the Demon. What is he doing here?

"Men of the Council," said Edesso, "the honorable Emperor Valerio has departed to tour our great nation and make the court's love for them well-known. In his stead, we must appoint a regent. I have a recommendation."

Gods, no.

"In his capacity as Maestro of the Treasury, he eliminated all the wasted expenses and brought a surplus that funded bridges and repairs throughout Imperial City and Anthania, and paid the legions that secured Khazidea and—as we speak—repaired the Wall."

Please, Mother goddess, do not do this…

"In his capacity as Maestro of Justice—just days into his term—he found and executed the murderer of the Lornodorsi. He has uncovered a far-reaching network of assassins, and sent the Imperial Guard to dispose of them. He charged and executed the Mud Bottom cannibal without enraging the people. He has excelled at everything he did. He is shrewd and capable."

And a demon.

"I ask that the Council declare Amaraeus No-Name the regent of the Empire in Valerio's absence. Do any of you have objections?"

"None from me!" shouted Bruno Seánus.

Anthea had gone cold. Councilor Durantus' uncertain brown eyes met hers. His lip trembled.

"Perhaps we should name Anthea Adamantus regent."

A few guffaws met Durantus' sputtered recommendation.

"The people loved Claudio," Durantus continued, "and they will love his lady-wife."

Amaraeus stepped forward. "Perhaps that is best."

He is playing mind-games. Amaraeus did not have a good bone within him.

"Much as I love the Adamanti, my councilors," said Speaker Edesso, "a woman cannot be regent. A woman has never ruled the Empire, nor sat on the Council."

"Empress Irena…" Durantus' voice was almost a whisper.

"A ruler for two months," said Speaker Edesso, "in the darkest times of the Empire, in the wake of the Yule-day Massacre and the murdered council and the Mad King from the east."

"She saved the Empire…"

"*Enough*, Durantus." Edesso's patience had evaporated. "I make a motion that we elect Amaraeus regent until Valerio returns from the tour. Any final words?"

Anthea bit her trembling lip. Her eyes watered. She didn't know if it was shock or discretion. Perhaps she knew that standing against Amaraeus would not end well for her.

Thirty hands went up. *Not even Durantus has the courage to fight him.*

A demon now ruled the Empire. At the sight of the new regent's gold eyes, Anthea shivered and stood up.

~

Melorra's blue eyes held the same unease as the morning. "Beloved," she said, "it is good to see your face."

Anthea could not fake a smile. She sat on the bed. "Amaraeus is the regent. I think our country is done for."

"I don't know why you fear him so."

"*Be a good judge of character*, my husband said. Now without him, I am dead. There is no hope for me, for us."

"He does not wish you harm, beloved."

The words angered her, she realized, but she wouldn't lash out at her one true friend.

"Besides, the Mother is afraid—"

Anthea made a hushing sound. She didn't need to hear about fire or earthquakes, or anything that frightened her at a time like this. She looked over at the priestess, took her white hand in hers, and gazed into her troubled eyes. The scars that ran across her flesh sent vicarious pain through Anthea's nerves. "Why did Lysandra do that to you? Why? She may be a lupa, but even lupas have reasons for what they do."

"I saw things." Melorra's voice was weak. "I saw things I still don't understand. I don't want to trouble you, beloved."

"Trouble me," Anthea commanded her.

"Ah, beloved, Lysandra and perhaps your son have become part of a dark cult. The Revered Sister of the Grand Mother Temple told me about it. They believe a black serpent will eat the world. They believe only he can face the Evil One. Perhaps the cult has a good goal, to fight the Deceiver, but their means could not be more wicked."

"The Evil One? The Deceiver?" More theology that Anthea did not care to grasp. "There are only gods and wicked men. That is what you told me." Demons are only fodder for tales, she heard.

"I've told you a lot of things, beloved. Do not trouble yourself. It does not matter. Lady Lysandra paid a Black Serpent to kill someone. I'm not sure who, or where. That is why I have these scars."

"The Magistrate of Korthos died of heart trouble…"

"Do not worry, beloved. There is no use to it."

Anthea's stomach growled. *Hunger will claim us before Amaraeus does. No matter what, we are doomed.*

CHAPTER THIRTEEN:
CLEARING THE NEST

Ferro No-Name, Marshal of the Imperial Guard

As he traveled the streets of the Suburro—seeing the starving skeletons huddled along the muddy streets—Ferro couldn't help but notice the glares he received. The red halfcloak made it clear that he belonged to the Imperial Guard. Many of these poor citizens—guttertrash, as he'd heard several Augusts call them—had nothing but resentment for the palace court. They thought Ferro pocketed their tax money, personally canceled the program of free bread, and brought starvation on them. Never mind that he'd once been wretched, too, a fatherless slave, a famous gladiator that no one paid. It was all before Amaraeus had rescued him, saved him from the filth, convinced Claudio-Valens to free him from his bondage and promote him to Imperial Guard. He owed everything to Amaraeus, and he would do everything for Amaraeus. The man was a chameleon, everyone to everybody, a thousand different faces. The palace was full of his friends and men that, like Ferro, owed him a life-debt. The enemies he had likely didn't even know his name. He said he wanted to create a better world, or to strengthen the Empire, or to punish his enemies. He said a lot of different things, and Ferro didn't know which of them he meant.

The man himself did not truly know who he was, or even what he was. Like Ferro he'd been fatherless, a baby left up to adoption by a mother who didn't want him. The new regent claimed that he'd visited the southron lands with the emperor Claudio and seen men with the same features as himself, that he was from a place of eternal summer, from an island that only the southrons knew about, ruled by a "queen mother" named Kandahei. But it was impossible to know when he spoke truth and when he used his lying tongue.

The guttertrash scurried off in a dozen different directions when they reached Benetto's Tavern. The building was as run down as everything else in the Suburro. Much of the wood had broken off or rotted away, revealing soot-stained brick. Amaraeus' orders were clear: *Kill everyone in the tavern, and everyone in the Serpent's Lair.*

When they entered the tavern, people screamed. Ferro had done Amaraeus' dirty-work too long to hesitate. The man had turned him cold.

The slaughter in Benetto's tavern was a red dream. At some point he awoke, drenched in blood and dripping all over. Heads and arms, or the rarer whole body, lay sprawled around the guttertrash den: men, women, even a boy. Immediately they threw tables, broke all the wine bottles in their search for the "secret door." At last, a guard hollered he'd found it in the wine cellar, and they rushed in together, finding themselves in a different world.

Right where the last red dream ended, it began again. A woman in a black dress begged for her life, but Ferro hacked her to death. One by one they looked through the rooms. Once again he woke from the dream, once again on alert, tense and nearly shaking. One by one he found the rooms empty. At last, he ordered them to turn around.

He was feeling nauseous. There was a strange scent and a heaviness to the air. In time, he found the door. But thirteen men in black leather were waiting for him.

The red dream, the dance of death, began again. Blood spurted everywhere but it was the guards' own. The men in black leathers were cutting them up, and dodging all their sluggish blows. A red dream, a red dream; a dagger pierced his chest and he fell to the floor. Time slowed. The blood was so warm, so wonderfully warm. When this red dream ended, there was nothing, only death.

CHAPTER FOURTEEN:
RED SHIPS

Anthea Adamantus

In the cool of the morning dark, Anthea stood on the balcony, shaking with hunger. The lack of food had weakened her. Famine's grim sickle would slay them all. She bit her lips and prayed.

What a fool she'd been to empty the palace stockpiles. She tried to help the people, but she did not. The only thing she did was anger the court and turn everyone against her. *The palace is a nest of vipers, and there is no one I can trust.*

Melorra's hand touched her shoulder. She had not left her sickbed since the injury. But here she was.

Anthea could sense her fear. What would the day bring? The rioting would continue until the people lost their strength. Then one by one, they'd die, and they'd turn into wild savages.

A pale glow touched the sea, rising upward. She did not welcome the summer sun and its heat. It would bake them like it baked the crops of Khazidea. In darkness, Anthea could imagine a different world. But now the sun—rising even now—would show the Empire's wretched state. Hunger had touched them all, and soon it would claim everyone.

As light dawned and the sky pinkened, an army of ships greeted Anthea's eyes. They were not Imperial war-galleys, nor were they the dhows of Fharas. Their crimson sails did not bear the eagle or the Four-Pointed Star. A white dragon was their symbol.

"Who are they?" Anthea muttered.

Melorra cried out and staggered back. *She is afraid.*

"Why are you afraid?" Anthea said. "Perhaps they are our salvation."

"My beloved."

Anthea turned her head. Melorra had collapsed onto her back. Anthea turned her gaze back to the dragon-ships, the army of the sea. "Perhaps the Mother has answered our prayers. Yes! Yes! The Mother has preserved us." She wondered if the hunger had driven her mad. But how could it not be the Mother's mercy? At their darkest hour, ships had come to port. Perhaps they had food. Perhaps they were servants from Heaven. Yes, yes, perhaps.

She would find out soon.

1050

CHAPTER FIFTEEN:
THE ONE

Anthea Adamantus

With the winter storms raging, and the giant waves crashing against Imperial City's breakwater, it was impossible to know how well Khazidea's harvest had gone. Perhaps Valerio Lucullus—last seen in Bregantium—would know better, but even that was doubtful.

In all, it didn't matter for now. The people were fed. The Redcloaks—as the citizens called the refugees—had brought food. Now, Anthea sat in her bedchamber, eating sweetbread and drinking a cup of rosewater. *I owe it all to the Redcloaks,* she thought, and yet now—two months after they'd arrived, Anthea had not met their leader, the now semi-mythical Lidda. Today, once she finished the bread, that would change.

In her younger years, she would—against the wishes of Claudio and the Imperial Guard—dress in a tattered gray cloak and wander the dangerous city streets. She had not done it for ten years, at least. But she had to see for herself. New Year's had come and gone. It was too long to still know nothing. She donned her cloak and left the palace without detection.

The streets of Imperial City were sopping wet, and water had collected between the pavestones. She could only make out a dozen people in Imperial Square—a tiny number even for winter. *Something's changed.*

She went on in the shadow of the Hippodrome. A poor man with no teeth sat hunched against the concrete wall of an apartment block. In his trembling, wizened hands he held a dish. Anthea searched her pockets. She found two copper aesa and a silver denar. She dropped them all in the man's dish.

"The One bless you!" the beggar called out, then coughed violently.

The One. What in Varda does he mean? "Signore," she said, "where has everybody gone?"

"They've gone to temple. Lidda is speaking."

"Where is the temple?"

As the beggar gave directions, a coldness settled into Anthea, a coldness that was more than the winter chill.

Through the streets of Imperial City she went. On many of the doors of the apartment blocks and houses, dragon symbols were painted in red. The sight unnerved her. But at last, she found the "temple"—what used to be an abandoned apartment building. A woman's voice echoed over the rain.

Anthea bit her lip, gathered all her bravery, and stepped inside.

They had demolished all the walls to create a giant space. Hundreds, probably thousands, of people packed into the room. It was so warm compared to outside, and the people had sweetbread or saltbread in their hands. *No wonder they come here,* she thought.

In the distance, far against the wall, was who could only be Lidda. The woman wore a long red cloak like her underlings, and her brown hair and milk-white skin contrasted starkly with her crimson spicer eyes. A gold necklace hung around her low-cut dress, studded with a purplish-black gem. A child sat on her knee, looking up eagerly.

"What is your name?" Her voice was silken-smooth.

"I'm Fredo."

"The One loves little children like you, Fredo. The Great Power will preserve you against the Enemy. And so will I, and my son, who love you just as much."

Anthea fixed her attention on the giant of a man looming over Lidda. The broad-shouldered Redcloak had his mother's brown hair and pale skin, and his eyes—though slightly reddish—did not have the color of a severe spice user. Clipped to his belt was a curved scimitar, inset with the same purplish-black stone that his mother wore on her neck.

"Do you wish to give your life to the One? Do you wish to serve Him eagerly, and receive the Great Power of His radiance, and stand firm against the Enemy?"

"Yes." Fredo's voice held uncertainty.

"And will your father and mother also pledge themselves to the One?"

The little boy's eyes watered. "I have no mother nor father. My mother died from being sick and my father died in the war."

"But you have a new Father now. Once you take the Red, you will be changed forever. The One will be your father and mother. What a gift that is."

There were a few claps. Lidda embraced the little boy, but he did not look happy. Anthea's heart broke for him.

"In the name of Joffa the Prophet, and Lidda, Queen Regnant of Ascalor," she went on, "and in the name of my son, Prince Ashur Dragonstone, I commend little Fredo into the arms of the One. You are now changed, an enemy of the Enemy, and a child of the One."

Anthea had seen all she could bear. She turned and headed out the door.

"Wait! Who is this in the grays? The One has sent you to us—"

But her words only spurred her to run faster than before.

In the grand hall of the palace, she found Melorra—long healed of her wounds, though now well-scarred—kneeling and saying her prayers. *My one true friend,* Anthea thought to herself. After the disappearance of the entire Imperial Guard, and the arrival of the foreigners who brought blasphemy and division with their bread, and the demon Amaraeus serving as temporary ruler, it was good to have a friend.

She turned her bald head and weary blue eyes to meet Anthea. "Beloved," she said. "Where have you gone? You are not dressed like an empress."

"I went out into the streets. I saw the woman, Lidda, and her son Ashur."

"Mother preserve us," Melorra breathed. "They are spreading their lies among the citizens. They have brought food, but they have deceived the people. I do not know what they want, or what they stand to gain from the deceptions they spread. Mother preserve us, they have brought spiritual poison with their food. We should command them to leave while we still can."

Anthea pursed her lips. "Ah, Melorra. The people of the Empire are god-fearers. They would never turn their backs on—"

"There is evil in the human heart," Melorra said. "You of all people should know, and I as well."

"Do you know where they are from?" Anthea said.

"I have searched earnestly for the place called 'Ascalor,' but I cannot find it on the most exhaustive maps." Melorra frowned. "There is something strange about them, my beloved."

"Of course there is, but—"

"Have you looked into the eyes of the Redcloaks? It seems there is no person behind them. Did you notice that with the woman Lidda?"

"No, but—"

"We must be cautious." Melorra had paled. "I've been writing letters to the Revered Sister, and she is gravely concerned. We should exile them."

"They've brought us food."

"And spiritual poison." Melorra's voice was nearly a hiss. "If we do not send them away, we will have erred in the sight of the

Mother."

Anthea wanted to hiss back, but instead she laid a hand on the shoulder of her only true friend. "Ah," she said, and prayed to the Mother that her servant was wrong.

CHAPTER SIXTEEN: WINDWALKER

Masimo Vorenus, Augur

Masimo called up Wind, feeling the sweet chill of magic prickle his skin, and leapt into the sheltered waters of the harbor. He skipped across the water. One step, two steps, three steps. Each step he fell further, until finally he collapsed into the water, soaking his clothing.

The greatest augur in history, the Windwalker, had such control that he could skip across the water for miles on end. At the pinnacle of his power, the Windwalker could fly like a bird. Masimo did not have his raw talent or powers of Wind, but he dreamed of one day becoming just as skilled. Wading through the chill waters of sea, Masimo found a hooded man standing there, clutching something his hands.

"Masimo Vorenus," he muttered and handed over a bound-up scroll.

In his wet, shivering hands, Masimo took the paper and saw it had an Imperial seal. When he looked up once more at the hooded man, he was already stalking away.

Shivering from the wetness and the winter chill, Masimo headed down the street. In an alley he paused, drew in a deep, sucking breath, and broke the hardened red wax. The scroll fell open:

Masimo Vorenus:

You are skilled, one of the best augurs in the Empire, and yet you are not a Maestro of the Collegium. I request that you travel to Korthos, bring back the lady Lysandra in chains or—if all else fails—as a head, for

an immediate reward of thirty gold libra and my
eternal gratitude.

Signed,
Anthea Adamantus

Thirty gold libra was enough to live comfortably for years, but
the real reward—in Masimo's view—was the gratitude of the
Adamanti. With the restrictions on Imperial seals and the horrid
punishments for attempting to copy them, Masimo had no doubts that
the letter came from the former empress. But Lady Lysandra was
married to her son Lucento Adamantus, so why would she want her
dead?

Below, there was a footnote:

Once you have reached the city, go to Phalcar Street and inquire for
Signor Metellus.

Masimo swallowed his unease and headed back to his quarters
in the Collegium to pack his things.

~

The skies let up, and the sun showed its face for the first time
in days. It was mid-afternoon and Masimo headed down the Path of
Tidus. He traveled several miles, drawing up a bit of Wind to propel
his journey. The augurs, by tradition, did not use horses, but could
often outpace the beasts if they drew up great amounts of Wind and
summoned up all their Speed.

Quarterstaff in hand, winged leather cap giving away his
identity, Masimo drew a bit more attention than he wanted. Though
most common bandits dared not attack augurs or magicians of any
kind, there were those who would hold Masimo's gift against him.

Twilight came, and the squalor that projected around Imperial City for miles had not abated. *The Golden Hen,* a roadside inn with a slanted roof and a boarded-up window, would be his home for the night. He hoped Animon the Wind-Lord would give him good company.

A serving girl brushed the floor absently. The innkeeper, a gaunt man with a thick dagger clipped to his side, approached him as Masimo scanned the room: a group of legionaries playing dice, a man in gray rags swarming with fleas, and a common lupa, her arms wrapped around a leather-clad man with shifty, untrustworthy eyes.

"An augur." The innkeeper smiled. "A pleasure it is. Not often we see the likes of you in *The Golden Hen.* What brings you to Saint Caron Village?"

So that's what they call this dump. "I am headed to Korthos—" *I've said too much,* he thought and bit his lip.

The innkeeper's eyes glinted, perhaps noticing Masimo's momentary distress.

"The maestra wishes to open a new collegium." *What do I have to fear from an innkeeper?* He cursed himself for being so worried.

"Ah." The innkeeper smiled again. "You will be treated well at *The Golden Hen.* We have a fine capon stew for three denara…"

Even during a famine, that is criminal.

"A glass of Korthian white for six aesa."

Still criminal. "I will have them both." He needed a good meal, regardless of the cost, and he had a feeling he wouldn't find better prices in this decrepit highway town.

The capon stew was meager, but he couldn't help but feel it was worth the price. The innkeeper had watered down the Korthian wine. As he ate, a man in a bright purple tunic and loose white leggings appeared. He had guards with him. A merchant, obviously. He greeted the innkeeper with a "Hail!"

The innkeeper nodded, then sneered at the girl with the broom. "Mara, put those wicked hands to use and stable the man's horses." As she scurried off, he once again met the merchant's eyes and smiled. "Where do you come from, good signore?"

"From Zarubad, and the wildman-lands, and a dozen other places."

Zarubad… that town was so far away it seemed mythical to Masimo, but if he followed the Path of Tidus he'd eventually reach the domain of the northman-king.

"What news of the north?" The innkeeper's smile was a thin veneer; he was estimating, calculating, sizing up this man like he'd sized up Masimo.

"*The River Runs Red* is the new favorite song of the troubadours. Raiders have been attacking villages, burning churches and monasteries and hauling away treasures. As soon as they see the Green Dragon on a sail, the Zarubes take what they can and flee…"

"A pity." There was no real pity in the innkeeper's voice.

"A pity for them, and for me," the merchant said. "No one wants to buy or sell. They're all afraid of the raiders. I've come back empty-handed."

Whatever interest the innkeeper had in him vanished. "Regardless, you will pay. Two denara for a room and four more if you want capon stew."

The merchant balked. "My, your prices are high."

"There is a famine," the innkeeper growled. "You've been with the barbarians far too long."

If the harsh tone offended the merchant, he made no sign. "The east hungers as well. But the people there are more worried about the Temple Massacre and the—"

"Enough chatter. Have a seat. Your food will be served when it's ready."

Masimo stood up from his seat and prepared for bed.

Despite the darkness of the chamber, sleeping was a near impossible task. The drunken soldiers shouted so loudly that it seemed a battle went on in the common room. The vagabond from before and his lupa had a room right next to his, and the sounds of their illicit deed prevented Masimo from thinking, much less sleeping. The whole place reeked of coal from the fire, or spilt wine and beer, but eventually—despite the noise and the overall discomfort of the place—Masimo drifted to sleep.

When the roosters crowed, he left without saying goodbye to the innkeeper. He had places to be, and he wanted to get out of *The Golden Hen*. It didn't feel safe. He breathed a sigh of relief as he once again traveled down the Path of Tidus, quarterstaff in hand and Wind at his back.

By the end of the second day, he caught the welcome sight of trees and grass, bunched though they were amid still more buildings and temples and public works. The roadside inn he found—nestled under the shade of oaks and boasting a fragrant garden—had both a better interior and a more kindly innkeeper. But as he once again stowed his things in his room, and looked through it, he noticed the letter he'd gotten from Anthea Adamantus was gone, and he remembered that the owner of *The Golden Hen* had a key.

CHAPTER SEVENTEEN:
THE RED MOUNTAIN

Anthea Adamantus

Against the wishes of Melorra—and despite her reassurances that Anthea, too, considered Lidda an enemy—she summoned the foreigner and her son to the Imperial Palace.

Lidda arrived with the grace and composure of a noble lady. Her long robe and easy gait made it seem like she glided in. Anthea, greeting her in the common room, managed a half-smile and a nod.

Lidda bowed deeply. "Your Worship. The people have told me much of your kindness. I do believe the goodness of the One shines from within you."

"Thank you." The words were slow to come from her lips, and devoid of truth.

Prince Ashur knelt before her. He, too, wore a red cloak, but his was shorter.

"You have saved us from the great famine." Anthea half-smiled again. "I thought I would properly thank you. And perhaps… learn a bit more about you and where you come from."

Lidda smiled in return. "Ah, yes. I will be glad to tell you the whole of it. Shall we sit?" It seemed more a statement than a question; she took a seat on one of the white couches. "Ashur, please leave the ladies to speak alone."

The solemn warrior turned and walked away.

Lidda's crimson spice-addict eyes reminded her of Lysandra, and it was an unwelcome memory. "It is so good to see you at last, my sweet." She removed a headpiece and her auburn hair unfurled like a waterfall. "The people of this land are so strange, yet their hearts are so good. I suppose I should have expected such hospitality and warmth from their leader."

"I don't lead them any longer." A full smile managed to creep its way across Anthea's lips. She felt warm, secure, in Lidda's presence, despite the red of her eyes. "Where is Ascalor?" She began the questions which—she hoped—would put Melorra and her own fears at ease.

"By sea, the journey took us months. The Devil sent storms and monsters and robbers to prevent us from reaching you. Thank the One, he did not prevail. We stopped in the Karthun and asked the *bey* for safe haven there. What were we thinking, asking the Sea Raiders for help! We were trusting in the One's providence, I suppose, and that is good; but so many have sided with the Enemy." Lidda's smile faded. "One by one we stopped in the Spice Cities. But the men of Fharas are vile and unclean, and drove us out. The padisha there ordered all the satraps to deny us shelter. In time, they will be destroyed. I swear it."

I wonder why the padisha was so inhospitable. The thought made her shiver. "And where is Ascalor?" she repeated the question.

"The southrons, as you call them, have some knowledge of us. Some have been to Ascalor. They call it the Red Land because the earth is colored like blood. Our land is perfect for growing flameweed. You call it Haroon Spice, because the runners buy it there, but you are mistaken. It comes far from Haroon, my sweet."

Anthea stayed silent, waiting for her to go on. She did not disappoint.

"Three years ago there was a great disturbance. The Red Land has always been hot, but the sun beat down like fire. The flameweed produced a wondrous crop that year, but the heat troubled everyone in the palace and in the whole city of Malkat-Ur. But the worst was yet to come."

Seeing the melancholy in Lidda's eyes, Anthea put a hand on her shoulder.

"There is a mountain just barely in sight of Malkat-Ur. All the mountains in Ascalor are red, but this is the only one we call the Red Mountain. Flame burst from it. For nine days and nine nights, ash and fire fell. The Fields of Jezrael once produced surplus year after year, but the air grew so hot that even the flameweed died. But the worst was yet to come."

Anthea withdrew her hand and clasped them together to comfort herself.

"Those that did not die in the flame and stone perished from starvation. Using the Great Power I brought them back to life. Service in the name of the One knows no death. The buildings of Malkat-Ur had either burned down or collapsed in the weight of the ash. I left into the red-hot sun, toward the Red Mountain. And the worst was yet to come."

Despite all the talk of heat, Anthea had grown cold.

"At the Red Mountain I paused. I heard a cry—half-beast, half-man; half-spirit, half-mortal; half-demon, half-god—and it echoed throughout the whole of Ascalor. Our people's fortune had vanished like water into the horrid sun, but I knew then that the Last Days were upon us. You see, my sweet Anthea Adamantus, I realized what had happened.

"The Devil has awoken on the Red Mountain. And for the men of Ascalor, and the whole world, and for you and me, the worst is yet to come."

The sudden remembrance of Melorra's dream sent a violent shiver through Anthea's body, and she gasped for breath. "My, what a tale you tell," she said.

Lidda smiled sadly. "And all the bread, all the rosewater, had been stored after a great surplus. We took every loaf and every cask onto the ships. My people—the ones I raised by the Great Power— do not need to eat or drink. Their deathless state is a gift of the One. You are the only one who accepted our gift of food."

I wonder why. She did not want to know the answer, at least not now. "Your people… the Redcloaks… they are not living?"

"My son Ashur, the Dragon Prince, is like you. So am I, Lidda, mortal like you. For ages, through all the generations of kings and queens on the Dragon Throne, a few have been gifted with the Great

Power. I am one of them. The Redcloaks, as you call them, are the Deathless. They obey only me, and I obey only the One. You should have no fear of them."

"The One," Anthea breathed.

Apparently she took it as a question. "The One is locked in an eternal struggle with the Many. The Devil is one side of Him, and must be opposed; the good side of Him has many names—Mazda among the nomads, Bashtar among the Fharese, Alabaster among your people—and that side of Him must overcome both the Devil and the Many. The One abhors images. The One despises all wines and intoxicating drinks."

But permits Haroon spice?

"The One is opposed to the Many and all those who revere Them."

"My beloved Lidda, I think I've heard enough." Melorra would not like this woman at all. Before Lidda incriminated herself further, Anthea had halted her. She wanted to like Lidda. She felt warm around her, safe. "You may come and go as you please. I shall like to hear more about your land, and your god."

Lidda's milk-white cheeks flashed pink. Anger touched her eyes and it was a terrible thing to behold. "Do not defile the One's name by calling him a god."

"I… I am sorry."

Lidda's snarl vanished. "I am sorry, too, my sweet. You are learning. I should not be so cross. But I fear I must go to temple. The citizens await."

As she drew up her cloak and turned to leave, Anthea realized she did not like what she said at all.

CHAPTER EIGHTEEN: BLOOD AND GLORY

Theon No-Name, Slave

The shadowcats darted at him. You had to start swinging soon as you saw them, or you'd get a neck-full of teeth by the time you raised your sword. He made two cuts, and two black jungle cats skidded behind him, leaving a trail of blood. The Imperial Arena burst into cheers, so loud that it shook the ground beneath Theon's sandals. Besides those little things, Theon wore nothing save his sword and buckler. Julian, his domino, said it impressed people more when he fought with no armor nor clothing, that it showed he could overcome just about anybody. And really, he could.

When the cheering died down, a girl screamed: "Theon, will you marry me?"

But the answer was no. The answer was always no. Domino Julian said he couldn't marry nobody because it would distract him from the arena. Sure, he could go to the whorehouses in the Suburro and the domino even paid for it, but he couldn't marry nobody.

The gates opened and out came Helmur Bloodaxe. At the sight of the tall, white, redheaded barbarian from Gad, the crowd broke into roars again. It was the final fight. They were using real, killing swords this time. The rivalry would finally end. Who would die? Theon, the dark easterner, or Helmur, the barbarian who was all rage and fury and no skill? Theon charged with his shortsword and Helmur pitched back his giant two-bitted axe.

Up in the Imperial box, the regent's eyes glinted gold as he watched them. Those orbs really got under your skin.

They exchanged a few blows, but the battle for Theon was like a dance. It was never a conscious thing, it was more a dream, a thing he did more through instinct than thought.

He only woke when the axe had buried itself in his chest. He drew in cold breaths, sinking into the dirt of the Arena, bleeding all over. The cheer was muted; perhaps they never liked Helmur after all.

When the barbarian ripped the axe out of his chest the pain was more than he feared, sending ripples through his mind and soul. The regent had left the Imperial box. The already-quiet cheer had faded to nothing. Bleeding on the floor he lay. *My life is ended.*

"Marry me, Theon!" the same girl shouted above the quiet.

Perhaps, it isn't my fame she loves after all.

CHAPTER NINETEEN:
ENEMIES EVERYWHERE

Masimo Vorenus, Augur

By the time he reached Bregantium, the rain and cold had given him a chill he thought he'd never break away from. Even while basking in the fireplace warmth of *The River Queen Inn*, Masimo couldn't stop shivering.

The three-story inn, overlooking the Grand Slave Market, had blonde barmaids walking by with platters of food and pitchers of ale, attending to his every need. He'd been spending as little coin as he could, and thankfully the mug of ale and the plate of fried trout cost a fraction of what that awful capon and watered-down wine had cost him weeks ago. It seemed the innkeepers were more scrupulous in the north. In fact, Masimo wondered if he liked it better in this supposedly barbaric land. Certainly, the men and women were not as well-read in Nustor and Patreus, or the Thenoan and Thartan schools of philosophy, and Masimo had no illusions of their ability to find Imperial City on a map, but they were good-natured, authentic folk, and—compared to them—the people of Imperial City were downright rude.

"An ale for you, handsome?" a rare brunette asked him, inclining a pitcher his way.

"No, no." Masimo smiled. He'd acquired the nickname Handsome, but he had no doubts that every man who walked in was called Handsome, and every woman Beautiful.

"Are you staying long?" she asked.

What a pretty face. It seemed a requirement to work at The River Queen Inn. "No, I leave tomorrow. To Paladium and then to Eloesus."

She paled a bit. "Ah, be careful, handsome. The wetlands are crawling with bandits. Stay on the main road and in groups. And as for

Eloesus… oh my, my dear, be careful there. Have you heard about the emperor?"

Masimo's eyebrows creased of their own accord. He guessed he was a patriot, after all. "What happened with the emperor?"

"He was in Sarpedris, some flyspeck village in the north of the province… a masked man made a run at him."

Masimo gasped softly. "And?"

"He survived, thank the gods. The assassin escaped… practically vanished into thin air. Some people say Anthea Adamantus did it so she could put her son on the throne."

Masimo had his doubts. "What is your name, signora?"

"Samara… And yours?"

"Masimo," he said. Before he could pursue her further, some distraction had taken her across the room to another person, to another Handsome.

He sat by the fire for hours and still, felt no warmer than when he walked in. He had begun to nod off. The noise of the chatting crowd was less disconcerting than any roadside inn he'd stayed at. He felt warm, comfortable, and, most of all, safe.

He dreamed he was the Windwalker reborn. He was flying on the back of the Wind he conjured, then dropping down and running across the Imperial Sea. Animon the Wind-Lord, the great eagle god, looked down on him from on high, approving of him. He was the champion, the best augur who ever lived. He was the Windwalker. No… he was better than the Windwalker.

"Listen to me!" A voice startled him and he looked back. A man in dark leather, holding a poison-slicked dagger, stood in the doorway. A serpent was embroidered in orange thread across his jerkin. "There is a dark-hearted augur here, a man who—by the wishes of his cruel domina, Anthea Adamantus—has conspired to kill the emperor. His name is Masimo Vorenus. If you patrons do not identify him, I will have no choice but to kill you all."

"There he is!" Samara was pointing at him, the lupa.

Masimo grabbed his quarterstaff. *Who is this? Who knows about this? It must have something to do with the letter I left behind...* There was no time to think. The man in leathers was springing across tables, sending pitchers and mugs of ale to the floor. The inn erupted into chaos. Masimo called up Wind, let it carry him a foot into the air, and then called up more Wind, propelling him down hard onto the assassin and slamming the quarterstaff onto his head.

But the assassin darted away, quick as a cat. Masimo thrust his hand and staff forward, and sent a gust of concentrated Wind that hit him like a punch. He flew against the wall as the screaming crowd ran by him.

There could be others. He is out of my way for now.

Masimo wanted nothing more to see him dead, but a man like this certainly would not come alone. He called up more Wind, darted across the common room and grabbed his pack. Then he bolted out the door, glimpsing—as he bolted out into the crisp night air—a pair of men in similar dark leathers running inside.

I am being hunted, he realized as he half-ran, half-flew across the bridge, going from the more slovenly West Bregantium into the eastern domain of the rich. His mission was compromised somehow. Though he had no idea who the men were, how they knew, or what the snake symbol meant, he was certain they were protecting Lysandra, and he was being hunted.

In time, he was out of the gate of Bregantium, zipping by the town watch as warning-bells rang. It was too bad that he had to leave. Of all the places he'd gone through this ill-fated journey, he had liked Bregantium the best of all.

The main road continued on. The southeastern portion of Gad awaited him. The marshes of Paladium and—perhaps—a small glance at Sanctum awaited him. Of one thing he was certain: there would be no extended stays, no popular inns or large cities.

The River Gad faded from his sight, the last rays of light left the sky, and Masimo was flying down the road at the back of Wind, away from Bregantium but knowing full-well he was unsafe.

~

Drawing as little notice as he could, taking the most obscure yet direct routes he knew, Masimo sped toward Paladium as the icy hand of winter slowly loosed its grip. Flowers began to bloom, sprouting their pink blossoms, and the smell of pollen filled the air. More and more the sun shined and the air began to warm.

It was a sunny day when Masimo reached Dorimer's Ferry. Masimo never heard of the village, but this stone-and-brick town, straddling the banks of the Hyber River, provided the same service as the more famous town of Paladris and its bridge to the southwest.

The town itself, built on upraised ground above the ferry, had an ancient look, like Old Town in Peregoth. A shrine of Hieronus, god of justice, which greeted him as he entered, did not have the domes and T-shaped structure of the other temples; it looked carefully reworked. Going further in, a statue of a warrior with a hammer bore the name *Dorimer* and—in an instant—history lessons at the Augur Collegium flooded back to him. Dorimer the Hammer had, hundreds of years ago, forced the death-god worshiping River Folk to renounce their faith on threat of execution, and revere Hieronus lord of honor above all.

Ah, Paladium. *Gods, is it hot.* It would get hotter, soon, and humid too.

In the small cobbled town square, a fishmonger hollered after him: "Pickled trout, just four aesa! Steamed crawfish, a bowl for only two aesa!"

Masimo made sure not to look up.

A woman shouted this time: "I've a gown and a tunic, only lightly used! Two denara for both! Signore! Signore! Hey! Signore!"

He was half-tempted to look up at her, out of pity, but he bit his lip and continued, finally making it across the square.

The quaint little town passed him by, and he descended with the road down to the river's bank. The ferryman had already left his hut.

"Signore! What is your name?"

Why does he want to know? "Signore, my name is my own concern. Tell me yours and perhaps I'll tell you mine."

"Mather. I don't rightly have a surname but men called me Ferry."

"I wonder why."

Mather looked confused.

Irony is often lost on simple folk. "My name is Arkos, and I'm returning home to Eloesus. I don't have a surname either, Mather Ferry."

"Well, Signor Arkos, I suppose you wouldn't want a hot meal of trout with my wife Varise before you cross the river."

There is nothing more I want than a hot meal and a warm bed. But an augur cloaks himself in the wind. "I must leave, Mather. How much is the ferry?"

"Well, my good signore, it will cost you two moons to get across."

Masimo's money had dwindled so far since the day he left. "The toll for the bridge in Paladris is only four aesa. Two denara is a lot for a country ferryman to ask, don't you think?"

"You aren't in Paladris, my good signore. You're in Dorimer's Ferry. As I said, two moons or you won't get passage." All the simple country politeness had vanished from his voice. "Say, that's an odd walking stick you've got. May I see it?"

"You ask an awful lot of questions for a ferryman." Suddenly Masimo was glad that he'd stowed away his winged augur's cap. "It can't be good for business to put your nose in others' affairs."

"Two moons." The grunted words and sullen glare meant he would tolerate no more.

Masimo flipped him the two denara. It was practically robbery.

When they reached the other bank, Masimo stepped onto the muddy ground. The sun was setting and the night chill was flooding in. Mather once again pushed off the dock, rowing across the swift waters.

"Goodbye, Masimo," Mather said, and—cursing his foolishness—the augur sped down the road toward the marshes, knowing some conspiracy was brewing but having no idea who or what it was.

CHAPTER TWENTY:
DARKENED HEARTS

Anthea Adamantus

At first, suspicion is merely a seed. But if watered and nurtured, it grows into a baleful tree. So it was with Issadore Lucullus, the too-young wife of Valerio. The gold-haired eastern beauty loved her husband's title more than she loved her husband—that, Anthea had already gathered. Valerio Lucullus was a brave man, a competent general, and not horribly displeasing to look at, but he was incredibly dull. It seemed—in these months that he'd been away—that Issadore's lovers provided a way to occupy her in her husband's absence.

Anthea's heart broke for Valerio. More than once she grew teary on his behalf. She had felt so horribly when she learned of Claudio's mistress. And though—before her ascension to the Imperial palace—she'd sold her body, she had put those dark days far behind her, and had remained faithful to her husband to his dying breath.

She reflected on everything in her private bedchamber, lying lengthwise across the couch and sipping absently at a cup of tea. Perhaps Valerio should know. Perhaps not.

Melorra's bald face and flowing blue robe was a welcome sight. Yet her sapphire eyes dripped with tears, and her hold on the shepherd's crook was weak. "My beloved."

More tragedy. I wonder if I can bear it. "What is it, my dear?"

"The Revered Sister sent me a letter. It has worst news I could possibly hear."

"Tell me."

"The sisters in Korthos are dead. All save one, who escaped." Her voice trembled as she wept. "The worst news, my lady, is that the murderers were soldiers. Soldiers in Lucento and Lysandra's guard..."

"My son had nothing to do with it." Anthea's own eyes responded in kind, filling with tears. "My son could never do such a thing!" She raised her voice to overcome the hint of doubt, to crush the seed of suspicion before it grew. "It is Lysandra, if it is anyone. He should have never married that eastern witch."

"Witch." Melorra's voice had calmed but it still trembled. "The Mother has put a prescient thought in your head, my beloved. The Elder Sister in Korthos suspected Lysandra of having magic ability. But neither the Theurge Collegium nor the Hierophant Collegium has her on their roster."

"Why did they murder the sisters?"

"Lysandra and Lucento claim it is because they incited rebellion—"

"Hush!" She spoke too harshly. "My son has nothing to do with this." But the seed of suspicion had been watered, and soon it would grow. "What shall we do?"

"Petition Amaraeus to bring back Lysandra—"

"Do not mention his name."

"I do not know why you despise him so." Melorra's blue eyes had infinite compassion, but no understanding. "Perhaps, he has his own good at heart. Perhaps, he is immoral, devoid of the Mother's love. But he has no ill intent toward you, my beloved. If he did, the Mother would have warned me."

Anthea felt weak. "Ever since Claudio brought him into our household, he has served himself above all. He has lied more times than I can count, and even the truth he speaks is disguised through artful words. Claudio told me to trust my heart, that there are snakes in the palace—"

"The heart is full of love, but the heart is not meant for thinking."

Anthea sipped her tea again. "The heart is meant for many things..."

"Perhaps you should ask Amaraeus. I know you hold hatred for him, my beloved. I know you believe he is a liar, a silver-tongue, but he is regent, and he can bring your son back to you and out of Lysandra's grip."

She thought of telling her the secret mission, of the augur who—even now—had gone to capture or kill Lysandra. But she stopped herself. "Accompany me."

"Of course."

~

The gold eyes of Amaraeus—especially now that he sat on the White Throne—unnerved her, even angered her.

"Anthea Adamantus," he said, his voice as smooth as oil. "The wife of the greatest emperor who has ever lived. The people love you so, and so do I. Yet I see you so very rarely. I had not expected this pleasure. To what do I owe it?"

"Amaraeus," she said, "You owe this pleasure to Lysandra, my brother's demon wife." It was so hard to read those bright gold eyes. "She has murdered all the sisters at their temple in Korthos."

"Then she must be punished."

Perhaps I can trust him. "I request—no, I beg of you—that you send a legion to Korthos, bring her back in chains for a trial, and my son back here in Imperial City."

She sensed something had changed in him. "My domina, you do realize that the barbarians have been besieging the Wall for the past many months. I do not have a legion to spare." *How quickly my hope evaporates.* "And we cannot have your son in Imperial City. Without him, how will Korthos be led? Shall we leave them like a shepherdless flock to fend for themselves?"

"There are many who would take his position as magistrate."

"Would you insult your son's honor so?"

"Don't talk about my son!" Anthea hissed. "If you had children, perhaps you'd understand. Lysandra is a demon, Amaraeus! Don't you realize that?"

"My domina, you must calm down."

Melorra's hand touched her shoulder.

"As soon as the barbarian threat is diminished," he intoned with irritating calm, "we may talk again. But if we brought Lysandra back in chains, or had her killed, what good would that do? It would turn the whole Andereon family against us, my domina. I know it pains you, but we must act wisely."

"A whole temple massacred…" The voice was more a sob than a statement.

"The sisters' deaths are a great tragedy, certainly." The smooth voice had no trace of distress. "But we do not have all the information. Perhaps Lysandra is no saint—"

Anthea laughed joylessly.

"—but we do not have all the facts. Could the sisters be involved in some rebellious activity? Priests have not always acted with good intent. The emperor's task is to maintain peace, not exact revenge."

"*You are not emperor!*" Anthea shouted.

"True," Amaraeus said. "I am regent. I apologize, my domina. I should not pretend that is so. But regardless…"

"A whole temple murdered!"

Melorra's grip tightened. A whisper: "*Calm, my beloved.*"

"We must swallow our pride. Your son must remain in Korthos, and his wife by his side. The temple massacre is a grave misfortune, but peace must be maintained."

"A whole temple!" Melorra was dragging her backward, now.

"Overcome this, Anthea. Overcome your anger. Do not blame me for the murder. As I said, swallow your pride. And be calm, or I will have the Guard escort you out."

"May the Mother have mercy on your evil heart!" Anthea turned and ran for the door. Melorra followed just a few steps behind.

The palace is a nest of vipers, and she is the only one I trust.

CHAPTER TWENTY-ONE:
FALSE LIFE

Ferro No-Name

A pinprick, a sharp pain, and a deep breath. Someone was pulling him out of the mud, out of the slime and muck of the pauper's grave. A woman in a red cloak stood above him. A gem hung around her neck, and Ferro couldn't tell if it was black or purple. Her eyes had the crimson color of a spicer.

When he stood up, he did not do it of his own volition. But he stood up and—though half-eaten by worms—remained on his swollen greenish feet.

"Child," the woman said in an accent she did not recognize. It dawned on Ferro that they were outside of Imperial City's limits where corpses were buried. "I have brought you back to life with the Great Power. In your closeness with the One, you can no longer tell deceit. Therefore I shall ask you once each question, and know the truth."

Ferro was only an indwelling observer, watching his own body. It seemed he was alive, but he didn't feel alive. He was cold, without feeling or thought, and he wanted nothing more than to resist this strange woman, but he couldn't.

"You were once in the employ of the Imperial Guard."

No. He said nothing, but the witch's crimson eyes bulged at the thought.

"You lie to me."

Pain rattled through him like a shock, and he wanted to cry out but couldn't.

"The Deceiver works in you. Repent and tell me the truth. You were once in the employ of the Imperial Guard."

Yes.

"Good." She still looked angry. "You knew the inner

workings of the Imperial court, of all who live in the palace."

Yes.

"You knew the empress Anthea Adamantus well."

No.

A half-snarl arose on her face but she did not shock him like before. Perhaps she knew that he told the truth. "You knew Amaraeus, the one they call Silver-Tongue."

Yes.

"You know his heart is dark."

Yes.

"Does he intend to assassinate the emperor?"

No.

The anger arose again. The pain shot through his body once more, unbearable, unimaginable, like every sinew and nerve was on fire. He tried to cry out but could not control his voice or body, only his mind. *Yes.*

"The Deceiver runs deep in you. You are full of his lies. Where may I find proof?"

I don't know.

"Who else knows about his wicked intentions?"

I don't know.

The half-snarl arose again and sent his thoughts scrambling. "Does anyone in the Council know?"

Yes.

One by one she asked about the councilors. When finally he said *Yes* to the name of Bruno Seánus, the woman shocked him harder than ever before. "Begone, child of the Deceiver! May the Many feast on your flesh."

His spirit left the body, and as he floated away, he thanked the Heavens he no longer had to face those red eyes.

Then his spirit soared hurtling back, toward the necklace, through the gem and inside it; and there he was, trapped in a cold black prison from which he'd never escape.

CHAPTER TWENTY-TWO:
DESPERATE MEASURES

Edesso Vitellus, August

"Men of the Council," Edesso began, "Augusts all, the spring has brought news to our shores. There has been an attempt on the emperor's life."

"Gods help us!" shouted Bruno Seánus.

"Yet the worst foe may be right in our midst. The Redcloaks have won many converts in the city. The woman Lidda has convinced a mob to deface statues and protest outside temples. Perhaps we should force them to leave."

"We must be cautious!" shouted Councilor Durantus. "The Redcloaks are two-thousand strong. An armed conflict is the last thing we need. And the people will remember how they brought them out of famine and hunger."

"More take the Red every day," said Nestor, councilor of Mud Bottom. "If we don't stem the growth now, we may never be able to stop Lidda and the Redcloaks."

"We should oppose them," Edesso said, "but we should do it intelligently. The priests feel unsafe and rightly so. Lidda defames the gods every night at 'temple.' She has captivated their minds with all this talk of the 'One.' Perhaps…"

"Perhaps she is not worth fighting." Councilor Seánus never failed to surprise him. "This 'One' she speaks of is as much an abstract concept as the gods. Why do we care what the people believe?"

"You speak like a Thenoan philosopher," said Councilor Durantus, and Edesso couldn't tell whether it was an insult or a word of praise. "Yet still, there is much to fear from someone who has such control over the people's minds. It is best to oppose her."

For once, Edesso let the conversation take the course it would. He was Speaker, but sometimes it was best to let the councilors show their mettle.

"I should want this matter resolved by summer," Councilor Seánus went on. "Regardless of what we decide, we should not want this hanging over our heads while we're away."

In the cool of the foothills, the councilors liked to forget about their worries. But those days were still long-off, and things could spiral badly out of hand if they did not resolve the matter of the Redcloaks before then.

"We could call in a legion to escort them away," suggested Marcello Kerius, councilor of the Ricci district.

"Amaraeus says they are occupied on the borderlands." Edesso finally decided to speak. "And he does not lie. I have a proposition. We arrest the Redcloaks, charge them with inciting rebellion, and ban this religion of 'the One' on penalty of death."

"It seems wise," Kerius said.

A few murmured assent.

"Unless anyone has a more fitting idea, that is what I propose. Who consents to the arrest of the Redcloaks, the execution of Lidda, and the banning of the religion of the One?"

By a vote of twenty to ten, the measure passed. Edesso smiled and left the Council House toward Amaraeus. Call Amaraeus a schemer or a silver-tongue, he had no love for the Redcloaks. By the time summer came and the Council left for their villas in the foothills, the Redcloaks and their lady would be a distant memory. Edesso was certain of that, beyond a doubt.

CHAPTER TWENTY-THREE: THE BLOODY KERNUNNA

Fredo Paladrion

Fredo loved the taste of rosewater, and he loved the taste of saltbread. That was the only reason he went to temple. Not that Fredo didn't believe in the One and hate the Many, but just months ago he'd been starving. After a barbarian killed Pa, he'd had no one. When they stopped handing out free bread, Fredo had been done for. Then Mother Lidda and Brother Ashur showed up, and Fredo had the One for a father.

When the bells started to ring, Fredo remembered it was a short run to Imperial Square. After Mouse and Dirt Boy and the rest of the gang abandoned him on account of the One, Fredo spent a lot of time near Temple. He ran, wondering what news there was, even though Mother Lidda said not to care about what happens in the physical world.

He bolted past the red dragon-painted doors, through the mess of people. When he got to the huge open space of Imperial Square in the shadow of the palace and the Hippodrome, there was a man standing on the lectern. He had a purple sash around his white robe. People were gathering around.

But Fredo could hear, above the chattering, that lutes and drums were playing. *Mother Lidda hates music.* Four bonfires burned on the four corners of the square, and priests of Kernunnos—dressed in animal skins and blue paint—were dancing round the flames and singing:

> *Spring is joy and winter's pain*
> *Come ye, come ye, come ye, come!*
> *The earth has drunk the pouring rain*
> *Come ye, come ye, come ye, come!*

The winter shan't return again!
Come ye Vernals, come ye, come!

If Mother Lidda saw this, she would fly into a rage. Fredo had forgotten all about Kernunna. It was strange how much he changed. Back when Pa was alive, he loved Kernunna. He'd gather a bunch of flowers and give them to Mara. He wondered what happened to her. He used to love songs, but Lidda said songs were a creation of the Many, and music was a distraction from going to temple.

The man at the High Podium was talking now. He was an old man, older than father had been, with gray hair and a wrinkled face: "Citizens of the Empire, a joint edict from the Imperial Council and the sitting regent Amaraeus: we hereby declare the Redcloaks and their leader, the witch Lidda, as enemies of the state. They will await trial and likely execution in Tiduscus."

There were a few angry shouts from the crowd, and a few cheers.

"The religion of the One is banned, and anyone who professes it is sentenced to death by hanging."

Fredo didn't understand. The One was his new Pa, and Lidda was his new Ma. Why would they do this?

"The Fortieth Anthanian Legion is coming if the Redcloaks attempt to resist!"

A few people looked back. Fredo did the same. Prince Ashur and a line of Redcloaks were marching down the road.

"Brother Ashur!" Fredo cried out.

Brother Ashur was big, a giant, and he had the voice of a giant, too. "What is the meaning of this?" Brother Ashur didn't talk much, but when he talked everyone listened. "*Why have you set up idolatrous fires? The Deceiver works in you!*" He shouted something to the other Redcloaks. They started running.

Brother Ashur drew out his big curved sword. The man at the podium turned and ran for the palace. The Imperial Guard, standing in front, turned to face Prince Ashur as he charged. He was half again their height. Ashur told Fredo at temple that his sword had special jewels in it called dragonstone, and that dragonstone could trap men's souls so that they could never leave the physical world.

That was scary enough, but what sent Fredo's nerves jittering was Ashur's amazing ability with the sword. The Imperial Guard had shields, but Ashur dodged their weapons like he was dancing, twirling and leaping around and preventing them from so much as cutting his cloak. When Ashur slammed his scimitar on an Imperial Guard's helmet, Fredo gasped; when Ashur slashed halfway through the same man's neck, Fredo turned and ran.

Everyone else had the same idea, fleeing down the nearest street. The Redcloaks had collapsed the fires and now held the priests of Kernunnos down onto the flame as they screamed. When Fredo gave one last cursory look, the Imperial Guard had broken rank and four of their bodies lay there; Prince Ashur's scimitar dripped red.

Bells were ringing from the towers—warning bells, the same they used for fires and barbarian raids—and, as Fredo ran down the street, more stamping feet echoed through the air. The legion with their war-eagle shields hurried in from the distance. *Who do I fight for? Who do I fight?* He turned and ran back, faster than ever, for Imperial Square.

The skies were blue and sunny, but sharp thunder clapped and blue lightning sizzled. Dancing streams of azure and white danced across Prince Ashur's scimitar and crackled. The lightning had come from the hands of a magician, an easterner by the looks of him. Prince Ashur seemed stunned, fumbling on his feet, breathless perhaps, but he recovered, and—scimitar still sizzling—dashed forward like a wildcat and clove magician's skull in two before he could react.

The other Redcloaks held the priests of Kernunnos down on

the smoldering fires, as they gave their last screams. The legion was near.

"This is the punishment for those who worship the Many and their idolatrous fires!" A woman's voice was crying out. Mother Lidda ran in from a side street, her red cloak flowing. "This is the punishment for those who spurn the name of the One, who blaspheme, who dance or play music or drink the Devil's water."

That is her word for wine, Fredo remembered.

"The One will overcome the Many!" Lidda screamed. "Such was told to Prophet Joffa as he made sacrifices in the Fields of Jezrael in sight of the Red Mountain. The Many are coming, the ones you call the legion. The One, in his great wisdom and mercy, has provided a place for us. Come with me, all you who worship the One, and we will return victorious. All those who refuse us, who waited behind, will be slaughtered as a blood offering to the One!"

She turned and ran. Her son joined her. One by one, two by two, ten by ten, the Redcloaks followed. In small groups, hundreds of citizens—after hesitation—ran after them. The legion was nearly in the square. Fredo was the last to follow. But still, he ran in the wake of the trailing red of the cloaks, deciding then to follow the One with all his heart.

CHAPTER TWENTY-FOUR:
THROUGH PALADIUM

Masimo Vorenus, Augur

Midges ensured that Masimo never had a moment of comfort. Sedges and bulrushes rose up along the wetlands of Paladium. Whenever a pitcher plant trapped something, Masimo cheered under his breath. Flies, midges, mosquitoes and all biting things deserved death. Painful deaths, preferably.

The villages offered a bit of comfort, but—since Masimo no longer used the main Imperial road—they were mostly backwater, with only two or three families in as many houses and huts, eking out a meager living on fish or hunting lizards. Far beyond, through progressively more desolate wetland, lay high mountains that none—as far as Masimo knew—had ever crossed.

Somewhere nearby—if these country bumpkins could be trusted—lay a thick mangrove forest where the "Saard" live, beast riders, worshipers of a serpent god, and likely superstition. But who was Masimo to criticize these beliefs that gave them fodder for tall tales, that stopped their children from wandering off, that perhaps in some strange way gave them purpose.

He was a week down the trail, running by the power of the Wind. The journey had begun to wear on him, though he'd packed little, and rarely grew hungry. The spring heat, on the worst of days, caused the air to waver, and to his surprise he thought of winter fondly.

A village—larger than the others he'd passed but still less than a hundred souls, built on an artificial hill—boasted a road marker. One pointed west: *EIGHT LEAGUES TO SOLACE.* Another went southwest: *NINE LEAGUES TO SANCTUM.* Another pointed the way he intended: *SIXTY-TWO LEAGUES TO THE BRIDGE OF PALLISTER AND THE VALE OF ISTEROS.*

When he turned down the proper road, a voice caught him by

surprise: "Are you going to Eloesus?"

He'd had enough of country bumpkins asking questions. Still, he turned. A legionary stared back at him. The horsehair-crested helmet and standard-issue shortsword was a refreshing sight. "Why do you ask?" Masimo would say nothing about where he went.

"The temple massacre in Korthos… the vanishings… the Red Return… the abomination set up in Heaven's Square."

"My business is my own." Masimo turned. *I am going into hell on earth.* It was too late to turn back.

~

Six more days at the back of the Wind, six more days through the wetland and the tiny villages built in muck. The ground ascended and the swamps fell away. The town of Pallister and its mighty bridge loomed ahead. The smoke of cookfires rose up from its soot-darkened buildings. The stench heralded the hive of humanity that was to come. The river Sulis was too wide to cross through augury, too strong to swim. He would go through Pallister as swiftly and quietly as he was able.

CHAPTER TWENTY-FIVE:
THE ASCENSION

Edesso Vitellus, August

"Praise the gods that the Redcloaks have left," Edesso said with a smile, though he knew the next item was far less joyful. "I have ordered all their ships burned. Though they have fled, I am sure we will find them and soon. And yet, the fair sailing has brought other news... of a different kind." He eyed the letter, its red-waxed seal already broken. "A letter from Thénai. The emperor Valerio is dead."

A few councilors gasped.

"He collapsed on his way to Korthos... heart trouble, some say, but the man was healthy and strong."

"I see Amaraeus' hand all over this!" snapped Councilor Durantus. "Who else could it be?"

"Amaraeus? Not a chance," scoffed Bruno Seánus. "You must look closer to home, my fellow councilors. His wife Issadore has taken up with that brigand Cosimo Odensa. Perhaps—"

"She's taken up with half of Imperial City, if the rumors are to be believed." Edesso's grave humor only received a chuckle. A pall had already settled over them. "Shall we raise Amaraeus to emperor?"

"There is no reason for us not to do so!" Councilor Donello snapped. "There is nothing to suggest our good regent had anything to do with this."

"It smells of conspiracy," muttered Councilor Durantus.

"And you smell of many things, Galleo." Donello's eyes lighted with wicked humor. "I have not said anything about it through all our meetings."

Edesso did not agree, but several councilors laughed at the jest and Durantus looked down. "Let us speak rationally, Donello. I see nothing wrong with Amaraeus. Though, I must say, Valerio's death seems suspicious and he *would* be the chief beneficiary. Who else in the

Empire would want him dead more than Amaraeus?"

"Your suspicions are unfounded, Edesso," Bruno dismissed him. "Have we ever known Amaraeus to be anything but loyal, competent, and good-natured? It is more than I can say for many of you."

Edesso frowned. The vague insult was unnecessary. "Shall we take it to a vote, or does anyone else wish to speak?"

No one did. By a vote of nineteen to eleven, Amaraeus was declared emperor.

~

Anthea Adamantus

It was the Mother's providence that, when Melorra told her the news, she knelt in her shrine clutching the silver figurine. The likeness of the Mother of all gave her small comfort, though it did not prevent her from losing her breath.

"I am sorry, beloved." Melorra's calm voice helped, too. "The gods' will are inscrutable to us mortals. But I assure you, my beloved, they have not abandoned you. The Mother wishes good on you, my beloved."

"And so often it seems she does not." Anthea's voice did not tremble as she expected. "It is good to have you with me, my sister." She stood up, and her old knees flared in pain. Melorra embraced her from behind, and Anthea reveled in her loving grip.

"The Redcloaks are gone," Melorra said. "Surely, we can thank the Mother for that."

Anthea turned and Melorra's tight embrace fell away. She looked into the priestess's warm blue eyes in all their infinite compassion and their unwillingness to harm. It struck Anthea that she had not hated Lidda as much as Melorra, even in spite of the Redcloaks' heretical religion. "Lidda told me the Devil has been born on a mountain. I suppose it is more of their gibberish, but her glib tongue has affected me."

Melorra's eyes glazed with a film of fear, and her bald white face grew whiter. "Ah," the word came like a cold gasp. "Their beliefs are false, designed to ensnare the weak and the impressionable. I do not know what the crimson witch intends with all this talk of the One; I read falsehood, or worse, in her eyes when she speaks of it. But as for the Devil and his rebirth, I fear…" Her voice trailed off.

"What?" Anthea spoke as calmly as she could.

"I rest in the palm of the Mother's hand. I feel her sadness, and I feel her fear… something has happened, my beloved. There is far more to fear than Amaraeus. In the Red Land something evil has begun. But Lidda—if her intentions are at all pure—fights the Deceiver with as much dark-hearted cruelty as any demoniac ever has in His unholy service."

"There are only gods and wicked men," Anthea muttered.

"A glib untruth, fed to the people by the Pontifex." It seemed Melorra did not wish to speak of this anymore.

"You told me that long ago."

"I spoke deceit," Melorra muttered. "And for it, I deserve to be flogged and cast from the Mother's hand. I told you that to comfort you, and by doing so I uttered the Deceiver's lies."

Anthea shivered. "Let's focus on what is before us. You do not deserve to be flogged. You are my sister. You are the only one I trust. We must survive Amaraeus together."

The half-derisive look Melorra gave her spoke wordlessly: *You poor thing, Amaraeus wishes nothing ill toward you, and it is not worth saying to you again.*

It could have angered her, but instead she grasped the Mother's figurine and uttered a prayer for them all. She, like Melorra, sheltered in the palm of the Mother's hand.

CHAPTER TWENTY-SIX:
A THOUSAND FACES

Amaraeus No-Name

"Silver-Tongue," the black-haired Eloesian said, once safely in the privacy of Amaraeus' bedchamber. He offered a velvet coinpurse heavy with gold. "Marcellus the Bregantine tells me he had a change of heart."

"He gave up fifteen libra." For all the strings he pulled and the puppets he played, Amaraeus so often did not understand people. "Why? He accomplished the task I set before him."

"He has left for the southlands in the company of a strange man. It seems the cold-blooded assassin has found religion, or something like it."

Amaraeus bit his lip to disguise his distaste. He took the coinpurse. "You may have five libra, Signor…"

The Eloesian looked offended that Amaraeus had forgotten his name. *So many puppets, so many strings.* "My name is Phadros, Silver-Tongue."

"And mine is not Silver-Tongue. Remember that, Signor Phadros. I hope you put the money to good use, and that you remember my goodwill."

"I could never forget."

The ten remaining libra would be useful, he was sure. It was enough to buy off anyone of middling means. "I suppose you have heard the good news."

"No…"

"That I am emperor. No longer am I regent."

"I thought you were Maestro of War."

"I am everyone to everybody. But now I am emperor of all."

CHAPTER TWENTY-SEVEN:
SERPENT QUEEN

Masimo Vorenus, Augur

North of Heaven's Bridge, in the town of Pallister, Masimo did not see a single tavern or brothel. Music was regulated to ensure no "erotic" southron influence, and dancing was discouraged. Temples outnumbered shops, and statues of Hieronus guarded every street-corner. If the rumors were true, a curfew after dark prevented anyone from leaving their homes. The exarch Orimer and his white-robed garrison of holy knights ensured that no fun or joy would be had.

But once—after lengthy questioning—Masimo crossed the bridge, and after a sign indicated he entered into Eloesus, everything changed. The familiar stretch of taverns, noisy inns, and brothels lined the main thoroughfare, and after so long in the staid, pious land of Paladium it nearly sickened him. The smell of cooking flatbread and a waft of dry Eloesian goat-cheese teased his stomach. A short distance away, a range of low cypress-covered mountains heralded the coming of the fertile Vale of Isteros.

But here Masimo was, in South Pallister as some called it or the City of Sin as they said derisively across the bridge. He had been to Eloesus once, but something had changed. The people looked down, not daring to meet each other's eye. He caught whispers of something called the "red return," and the vanishing of peasants and slaves across the country, and of the murder of the emperor Valerio. Underneath the veneer of deference and timidity, something dark was at work in Eloesus. It would take calm words and trust before Masimo found out what it was.

As soon as he could, Masimo diverged from the main road, and found himself in a world of grazing goats and sheep, as far as he could get from the packed road and the thick summer heat.

He was three days down these rustic dirt paths, and the sun making its final descent, when a goatherd in a loose white tunic hopped over a fence to approach him. "I don't like the way you're headed, signore."

Masimo turned to face him, peering deep into the bumpkin's strangely self-assured brown eyes. "I'm not sure I like the reprimand, Signor Goatherd." He meant the appellation as an insult.

The goatherd smiled in return. "You have the look of a wind-caller. The Serpent Queen of Korthos has heard that one of you is coming to kill her. She's killed a few dozen that she suspected, and not a fourth of them were wind-callers, nor even godtouched at all, neither."

Wind-callers, godtouched. Goatherds here had a lot of strange words for magic. "My business is my own, goatherd. I'd keep your tongue still. There are a lot of men who use these roads that would cut it off."

"You don't got to fear me," the goatherd said, cheery as ever. "It's the Black Serpents you've got to fear."

More peasant superstition, perhaps.

"None of we lowbloods love the Black Serpents, but soon as we speak out against them, we vanish. And what with the Red Return, and the massacre, and all the other terrors, you'd best watch yourself, signore. You're a godtouched, I can smell it, and maybe a wind-caller too. I'd turn back soon as you can. Either that, or meet at the Twin Palms Tavern in Caperna at sundown tomorrow, where Signor Metellus is waiting for you."

Memories of Anthea Adamantus' letter flashed back to him. Instructions to meet Signor Metellus. "Caperna." The word was more a mutter than a question.

"Keep following this road, and you'll come to it." A knowing smile brightened the goatherd's face. Masimo did not return it. Instead, he ran.

By noon of the next day, he reached Caperna, a small village in sight of the mountains. The Twin Palms Inn had one story, and when Masimo got inside he realized what a dark and shadowy place it was. He ordered a glass of Korthian red, marveling at its cheap price here—what cost a denar in Imperial City was only two aesa at Twin Palms—and the rich wine tasted just as good, if not better. It went well with the leg of lamb and the thick flatbread. For a while he forgot his troubles. But soon dawn came, and with it, a hulk of a man in chainmail who could only be an Imperial knight. As soon as they exchanged glances, it was evident he recognized Masimo for who he was.

In an instant, he realized it could all be a trap; what if the man at the roadside inn had broadcast the contents of the letter to Lady Lysandra, and this was all a setup? What if this wasn't Sir Metellus at all, and he intended to kill Masimo right then and there? He gripped his staff tighter. *What if?*

As the knight strode over to him, the bluish metal of his sword stood out against the polished gray of his chain shirt. He wielded a sword of adamant, a priceless weapon beyond the means of all but the wealthiest of the wealthy. Anthea Adamantus provided it, perhaps. Anthea, or Lysandra. He'd find out soon.

The mountain of a man took a seat. "Masimo Vorenus," he said in a too-loud voice. Perhaps sensing Masimo's concern, he added, "The keepers of the inn are no friends of Lysandra or the Black Serpents."

The innkeeper, a brunette, waved at Masimo, and he sickened.

"With the news about you in every Serpent's Lair, it's a wonder that you've made it this far. They had an assassin on every street in Pallister, but you had just gone. Her men in Korthos are ready for even the slightest suspicion."

"I suppose it will be an impossible task, then."

Signor Metellus was large, but every bit of it was muscle. Though his name and hook nose proved his Imperial lineage, the thick brown mustache he wore seemed more Paladian than western. Masimo realized he missed the west. "Do you know," Signor Metellus began, "that my father served Claudio Adamantus in his personal guard? Everything Claudio set his mind to, he accomplished. The conquest of Khazidea was all due to him. It seemed to my father that the very fabric of life bent for Claudio, that he was truly the son of Hieronus himself, the best-favored of any man to ever live. It is that favor—and the blessing of his wife Anthea—that we rely on."

Masimo felt his shoulders shrink. Such divine favor could not be depended on.

"The spirit of Claudio-Valens Adamantus watches over us, Masimo. I have no doubts he rages against Lysandra on behalf of his son."

"His son?" A coldness settled over Masimo, a realization that bad news was coming.

"The Red Return. Did you not hear?"

"No." The word came like a gasp.

"Lysandra murdered Lucento-Valens after they returned from the funeral. She offered his still-beating heart before the demon shrine in Heaven's Square."

"Gods!" Masimo wanted to vomit.

"She now lives with a murderer named Eightfingers." Signor Metellus' voice had none of the quivering emotion, the sickness, that Masimo felt. "The Elder Sister of the Mother Temple there spoke against it and commanded the people to rise up. You've probably heard—"

"The temple massacre," Masimo finished, his voice weak and cold.

"Yet there are elements in Eloesus that oppose Lady Lysandra. It is them that we will rely on. That, and the spirit of Claudio-Valens—whom most Eloesians still view as a god."

"How will we get into Korthos?" Masimo asked in a hushed voice.

"Magic power runs in your blood," said Signor Metellus. "I know little of you or your kind, but I am aware that you can sense each other. Be warned, augur, that Lady Lysandra is a magic-weaver. It is believed that she is a theurge—uninitiated and untrained."

A lady like Lysandra would have no scruples, nothing holding her back from tapping into the great dark, from reaching into the forbidden void and receiving power from shadow. In time she would go mad and destroy herself, but not before she destroyed everyone around her. "That is bad news. But if I am prepared, I can hide myself if I try. It only complicates things."

"Lady Lysandra believes I am her friend," Signor Metellus said. "I will take you to Thénai, and from there, my friend Tyros will transport you into the Korthos harbor. You will hide in the hull until you are close; then you will hide in an empty barrel. The Lady Lysandra awaits a shipment of wine. I will meet you in the cellar."

Masimo nodded. *What have I gotten myself into,* he wondered. But he had gone too far, tried too hard, and risked so much to turn back now.

"Rest yourself." Signor Metellus wore a half-frown. "We ride hard tomorrow. By nightfall, I want you on the ship. You are a brave man, Masimo, a patriot, and the whole Empire will thank you when this is done."

But despite all the kind words, Masimo was trembling.

CHAPTER TWENTY-EIGHT:
TRUTH

Melorra, Beloved of the Mother

Melorra had pledged herself to Anthea in a bond of love, and that love grew stronger every day. Every time Melorra saw Anthea sad, her own heart broke. She had not told her everything she knew, just so that she could spare her the misery. The letter from the Revered Sister had told her more, so much terribly more that she dared not utter to her beloved. She eyed the letter, lying on the desk:

To Melorra, whom the Mother entrusts with sister Anthea's loving-care:

The news I bear could not possibly be more terrible, nor could it break the Mother's heart more deeply. Great evils are stirring in the wide world and though the gods shelter us in their radiance, the children of the Evil One surface more proudly and openly than they have in remembered time. The great tragedy I wish to inform you of has taken place in Korthos.

Not long after Lysandra Adamantus returned from Imperial City, her husband Lucento-Valens was killed and offered to a demon shrine she had set up in the religious center of Korthos. She proclaimed herself Lysandra Andereon again, saying she despises the name Adamantus and hates all who bear it. Lenorra, Elder Sister, denounced them and encouraged the people to rebel. Now the Mother Temple has been massacred.

After lamentation and grief, another horrible revelation:

Lysandra is a black theurge, a practitioner of the dark arts.

It was more than Anthea Adamantus could bear; more, even, than Melorra herself could bear. And as far as she knew, the Redcloaks were still alive and in hiding. Perhaps, they were not the worst enemy. Perhaps, Lysandra was. But it seemed when she communed with the Mother, and felt—in meditation—as the goddess herself felt, near all the trepidation centered on Lidda and her strange religion, and the Red Land from which they came.

The summer heat warmed her bedchamber well, and outside the brilliant blue skies brought her small comfort. With the departure of the Redcloaks it seemed that things had returned to normal, or at least some kind of normal. Few shed tears for Lidda's departure, and those that did had gone with her. Amaraeus had sent scouts throughout Anthania to find them, and sent heralds to proclaim that whoever gave her shelter would face execution in Imperial Square. But though Melorra was certain beyond a doubt that Amaraeus meant no express harm to her beloved sister Anthea, she had little trust for the new emperor. The Mother did not fear him as much as Lidda and the folk of the Red Land, but more than once Melorra had witnessed his glib tongue and his falsehoods. He served himself first and foremost, and there was nothing to trust in those gold eyes, but those gold eyes held no love for the Redcloaks and that alone endeared Amaraeus to her.

How large was Imperial City, stretching into the horizon. As a girl Melorra had been abandoned, a six-year-old wandering the streets of Mud Bottom, easy prey for any wicked man or slaver. Then the Revered Sister herself visited the squalor, and Melorra had thrown herself at the priestess's feet. Severa Lucianus, the lost girl, had found a new name, a new life and a new purpose in the Mother's service. She had found the love of the goddess and had determined to spread it wherever she could.

She sensed Anthea behind her; the love-bond had grown so strong.

"Melorra," the former empress said. "I hope you pray for Lysandra's downfall."

"I pray that justice is served for all of us. I pray that the goddess's love be shown onto all of us."

She looked back to find her beloved's eyes running over the letter as it sat openly on the desk. Shock was dawning on her beloved's face. Shock, and horror.

"Beloved. Do not read that! It will only trouble you!"

Anthea took a step back, nearly tripping on her gown. "My son. My son is dead. My only son…"

"You have another." Melorra immediately knew she had chosen the wrong words. They stuck into Anthea like a knife, caused tears to form in her noble eyes. "I have spoken wrongly. I am sorry, my beloved."

"The world is full of snakes and vipers. And even the one I trust does not tell me everything. Perhaps I should not trust you, either."

"Beloved!" Melorra nearly screamed, but Anthea was on her way out of the room. *I should not have mentioned Claudian,* she thought, and began to cry.

CHAPTER TWENTY-NINE: A PROPOSITION

Helmur Bloodaxe

After he killed Theon, Helmur had no real rival. Of course, he wasn't surprised a bit at how it turned out. Theon was all skill and art, and no power. These southlanders were soft, he thought, as he walked the streets of the Suburro. They'd never lived through a winter like the "barbarians" had every year in the north, and they hadn't survived the clan wars that broke out every decade or so, nor the sacrifices to the Blue Dragon every third winter when they asked him to grant his warriors the strength of his frosty breath. But now he was here, in the baking hot, stinking southland capital, thousands of miles from the land he knew.

Past *The Lily Garden* he went, the brothel where his friend caught the Bumps; past *The Fertile Land*, a brothel of only Khazidees; *The Silver Candlestick*, full of milksops and just as filthy as *The Lily Garden*; and then a stretch of taverns, spice houses, and boarded-up buildings where the homeless lived with rats. The thane of Helmur's clan would have sneered at all of it. There were no brothels in the Land of the Blue Dragon; there were slave-girls, and there was your wife, and with all the wars outside your clan and within, a real warrior had little time for either.

Finally, he came to the tavern: *The Golden Cup* was sandwiched between two boarded-up houses. The door was half-open. Helmur could tell that a red dragon had been painted on it once, but it'd been scrubbed off. *Damned Redcloaks.* That woman, Lidda, had the look of a witch in those red eyes of hers. Helmur once listened to her talk, and for all her hatred of wine and beer, it seemed she had nothing against Haroon spice, which any sane man knew was worse.

Devil's water, my arse.

When he entered *The Golden Cup*, it was mostly empty. Only the barkeep and an unkempt, homeless-looking man in a tattered gray cloak were inside. But instantly the barkeep's copper eyes widened and he said, "My signore, Helmur. Whiteskin, some call you, or redbeard."

"Helmur will do just fine," he growled, and the barkeep shrunk back. People around the Suburro had learned not to test him.

"My good signore, our luxurious Blue Room has been prepared for you. My cook is preparing what he calls a 'surprise stew.' It will be served with a goblet of white Korthian wine, and a bowl of—"

"Enough!" Helmur growled again. "Show me the way."

The barkeep shrunk further back. "Yes. Yes, signore. Of course."

The "luxurious" Blue Room was anything but luxurious, and barely blue. The blue paint on the wall was peeling, and a wet spot on the roof dripped onto the table. Across the table from him, a man in a cloak rested his reddish-brown fingers on the dirty wood. This was the man who'd been sending him letters, the man who told Helmur he had a job for him, and that he could offer him anything he wanted.

"I wonder why you chose such a disgusting place when you claim to be rich," Helmur said through gritted teeth. "Who in their right minds would come here?"

"My thoughts exactly." His voice was smooth as oil. "Surely, you have heard of the Redcloaks. The so-called 'queen-regnant' of 'Ascalor' and her son Ashur. You've heard all her blasphemous talk of the One and the 'Devil' and the 'Many.'"

"I don't talk to a man when I can't see his face."

"Ah, the fire of the northerners burns in you. A legendary hot temper, like the berserkers. You will see my face soon, once the f—"

"I am not a berserker. If I was a berserker, you'd be headless by now, my good *signore*."

The barkeep brought in a bowl of walnuts, and two chipped

wineglasses of lead. "Your surprise stew will be ready soon, my signores."

"I don't want your surprise stew," Helmur said in an angrier tone than was perhaps necessary. "I hate being surprised, and judging by the decor here, the 'surprise' may well be rat-meat."

The hooded man chuckled. The barkeep let out an offended gasp. "Very well." He slammed the door behind him.

When the man lowered his hood, and the yellowish eyes of the emperor looked back at him and—around his woolen black hair— the gold of the Imperial Circlet glimmered in the candlelight, a chill went through Helmur, and he knew from then on that he'd best guard his tongue.

"Your Worsh—" Still, he could not bear to treat a southlander with such respect. "Signore."

Helmur thought he slighted Amaraeus, but the emperor instead smiled from one protruding ear to the other. "Ah, Helmur. Your fiery temperament will serve you well. You are the best gladiator that Imperial City has. The so-called 'prince,' Ashur Dragonstone, is honorable to a fault. We will challenge him… the Empire against Ascalor, the One against the gods, the old against the new. We will do our best to tip the duel in your favor."

"I need no trickery!" Helmur snarled. "I will fight man-for-man on equal footing. If I fight at all. And that, signor emperor, is still a question.

Amaraeus smiled, as if he expected it. "My good Signor Helmur, in exchange for you eliminating the threat of Ashur, the Imperial state will give you a mansion of your own. In the foothills of the Goldenhorns there is a village of sorts, Paradise Gardens, and—"

"No."

Amaraeus continued as if Helmur hadn't objected. "—a man of the August class, Lucus Albodoris, has an estate called White Lion Villa."

"N—" He gave up resistance and let him talk.

"The Albodorsi have usually been good, god-fearing Imperial citizens, but Lucus has sheltered the Redcloaks in his estate. I'm not sure the cause of his change of heart. If my plan works as well as I expect it to, you may have White Lion Villa for yourself in exchange."

When Amaraeus had provided a sufficient pause, he said again, "No."

Amaraeus' smile vanished. "What do you want, then, good signore?"

"I want you to stop calling me signore, first of all."

"It shall be done."

"I want freedom, to no longer be a slave. But it's more than that." He picked a toasted walnut in his fingers, and crushed it to dust. "I cannot be free when I live in this city. Freedom is running through the land I know, through *Guthrekat,* with my clan in the service of my thane. I want to go back to my homeland. That is what I wanted. That is all I have wanted, ever since I came to this sweltering pig sty."

Amaraeus' smile returned, and Helmur wasn't sure he liked it. "If that is what you want for a reward, then that is what you will get." He took a deep sip from his lead goblet, set it back down, and drew the hood once more around his face.

Helmur took a sip of his own, then spat out the putrid, watered-down wine.

CHAPTER THIRTY:
JOFFAT-UR

Fredo Paladrion

It was dawn and everyone at the White Lion Villa was gathered around Mother Lidda for temple, listening in the morning cool. Signor Albadoris was with them, wearing a red cloak of his own, and sitting cross-legged like everyone else. During temple, there was no August or slave, only children of the One and—outside—servants of the Enemy.

"Oh, my blessed children," Mother Lidda said. Her giant son Ashur towered above her in his bright red cloak and dragonstone-studded saber. "The One will preserve us all. He has called you out of the grip of the Many, and now you are warriors against them. Praise the One that abhors images, that detests the water of the Devil, that urges all of you to take up sabers and spears. Tonight, we have a lesson. And then, the One has a great task for all of you... one that will change this land of the Many forever. What a gift to see all of you in your red cloaks, to see that you have put aside the Many and their idolatrous fires, that you have changed from evil to good, from night to day."

A few cried out, "The One is mighty!" and Fredo joined in a half-second late. He couldn't wait for Mother Lidda's lesson this morning.

"Children of the One, I tell you an old story of Ascalor. A thousand years ago, the prophet Joffa danced in the flameweed fields of Jezrael in sight of the Red Mountain, where long ago the Devil— aspect of the One though he is—had been born the first time, and shortly thereafter, overcome. He was a man of seventy-seven years, and lamented that he had no children of his own. But as he danced in the fields of purple buds, he saw a little child playing alongside him. A thought occurred to him, that the One had sent this child to him because he had none of his own. He looked to the Red Mountain, and a voice said, *No, that is not why. Bring him to me, to my summit.* And the prophet Joffa took the child with him up to the highest point, to a great crater where, far below, fire can still be seen. And the voice said, *Throw him in,* and the insolent child struggled, but at last Prophet Joffa did so. And the One was happy. But you see, my fellow servants of the One, there was more to be done." Mother Lidda's smile was joyful, but the story saddened Fredo, and even scared him. "The One told Prophet Joffa to throw himself in the mountain. And with great gladness, he did so; and in the smoldering fires of the Red Mountain, he became one with the One." A few templegoers gasped. "But it is a happy story, my fellow servants. Sometimes, as a child of the One, you must sacrifice yourself. You must revel in the path the One demands of you."

"The One is mighty!" shouted Gaio, a man who'd been homeless before he met Lidda.

But the rest of the templegoers seemed less pleased with the story.

"The great goodness of Lucus Albadoris has given us a new home, which—for now—prevents the defiled servants of the Many from destroying the good servants of the One. The town of Malkat-Ur in the land of Ascalor has burned away. But now, in honor of the prophet—hero of today's story—I declare that the White Lion Villa shall be called Joffat-Ur, a new home for the children of the One."

A few more cheers echoed throughout the morning cool, and Fredo was one of them. But the sound of galloping horse echoed too, and when Fredo looked back, and a man in common Imperial clothing was riding toward Mother Lidda, he had a feeling something very bad was about to happen.

"Queen Lidda of Ascalor! I bear a message from His Undying Glory, Emperor Amaraeus."

Lidda's face pinkened. "You interrupt temple? Oh, you servants of the Many hold nothing sacred. You blaspheme. You declare that one of your own has undying glory. You—"

"Let me speak!" the rider snapped. Fredo's neck-hairs stood

on end; none here would ever speak so impudently to the One's own priestess. The rider opened a scroll. "Emperor Amaraeus asks that a trial be held. That, a week from today, in Imperial City, the honorable Prince Ashur Dragonstone—champion of the One—faces Helmur Bloodaxe, champion of the gods. Should Prince Ashur Dragonstone win, the Redcloaks may inhabit Imperial City for as long as they wish, and the religion of the One will be established as the faith of the land. Should Helmur Bloodaxe win, the Redcloaks may choose exile to Ascalor or execution, and the ban on the religion of the One shall remain."

The redness of Lidda's cheeks faded. "Ah! The One is good to us, my sweet children. In time immemorial, the priests of the Many and the priestess of the One fought in the streets of Ascalor. Blood flowed in the streets but it was not that of Priestess Rebah. So as it was, it shall be now. We accept your challenge, defiled servant." She was smiling at the rider, now. "When Ashur's saber drips red, all images shall be smashed, and all the bottles of Devil's water shall be emptied. The One has blessed us. The One is mighty!"

"The One is mighty!" the templegoers repeated at a shout, and Fredo was among them.

Moments after the rider had gone, Mother Lidda spoke again. In some point of the confusion of the lesson and the exchange with defiled servant of the Many, the Redcloaks had procured bowls of black liquid.

"A thousand of you have been chosen." Lidda's voice sounded cheerful, but something had changed. "From a city of incomparable size, an inkling have sworn their lives to the One. A pity that you live in such a vile nation, unclean and filled with images and idolatrous singing. It is all secondary, though; for you have chosen the right path in a country that has chosen the left. But your transformation is not complete! To become servants of the One, his

Great Power must fill you. This drink of boiled roots will fill you with his strength. The One is mighty!"

"The One is mighty!" a few repeated, but Fredo did not. Ever since he caught sight of those bowls, a nervous feeling began to surface in him, a feeling he did not like one bit. For the first time in days, he had an urge to turn and flee. But the Redcloaks surrounded them, and Mother Lidda did not tolerate disobedience.

One by one, the templegoers drank the black liquid. Lucus Albadoris drank first. A minute later—by the time they had gotten halfway down the row—he began to scream and shake. Eventually, he collapsed.

Fredo's heart was racing, now. A few of the templegoers went willingly. But Fredo was not as passionate a disciple of the One. Tears welled in his eyes, and he thought maybe that Dirt Boy and Mouse were right, that Mother Lidda was insane and maybe evil. He remembered the bloody Kernunna and thought of Pa and how much he loved the gods, and Ma too. The tears were streaming down his cheeks when the Redcloak shoved the bowl to his mouth. He opened wide, but did not drink.

The foul, bitter root-water burned his mouth as he held it there. Mother Lidda was smiling, but it was a she-wolf's smile now, he realized. Fredo had made a terrible mistake, coming here. He wondered if this had been Lidda's plan all along.

Mother Lidda was holding up her hands, and twin nimbuses of gold-white light circled around them. Lucus Albadoris gasped and sat up, but Fredo had a feeling he wasn't the same, that maybe he wasn't Lucus anymore, at all. Others gasped and stood up. By now the last of the templegoers had swallowed the poison, but Fredo still hadn't swallowed.

"Servants of the One, you will no longer know death."

More stood up, and finally Fredo couldn't handle the harsh bitter poison anymore. He spat it out and began to choke.

Lidda regarded him with her terrible red eyes, glaring. Her cheeks were pink again. "Child Fredo. Why have you not done as the One commands?"

"I don't want to die!" Fredo wept.

"You will not die, Fredo. You will become deathless, a servant of the One."

"A servant of *Lidda*!" He flew to his feet and bolted away from Lidda, hoping to dodge between the Redcloaks' legs. But a firm hand caught him by the shoulder; it was Lucus Albadoris, and Fredo saw Lidda's eyes behind his own.

"You lie, child!" Lidda shrieked. "You are a servant of Asura, the Prince of Lies, and your heart still clings to the Many. You are a friend of the Enemy, and an enemy of the One."

"I am!" Fredo half-shouted, half-gasped, though he didn't know why he did or where he got the strength. "I serve the Many. I want Ma and Pa! You aren't my mother, Lidda! I want my real mother."

"Your father is Asura, and your mother is Asur'ashan. You are not a fit servant of the One. Kill him."

Not a fit servant of you, he thought. When he looked down, a sword-blade stuck out through his chest. He was bleeding. *Better this than service to the One.* His knees hit the wet earth. *I am a servant of the Many, to the end.*

CHAPTER THIRTY-ONE:
THE ARRIVAL

Masimo Vorenus, Augur

In the hull of *The Sea Queen*, Masimo lay in an empty barrel. They were an hour from the harbor of Korthos, or at least that's what the captain Tyros said. Lysandra, for all her apparent change of heart, had not overcome her legendary love of wine. Perhaps that was the only thing that remained the same from the Lysandra Adamantus everyone thought they knew: now a theurge, and—by all accounts—a practitioner of the dark arts, an unscrupulous magician that reached into the dark void for its incredible yet maddening power; a murderess, killer of her own husband, and—as Signor Metellus explained—one who offered his still-beating heart before a vile demon's shrine. Masimo's mission was important to Anthea Adamantus, he was sure, especially if the dark news had reached her. But his mission was important to the people of Korthos, certainly oppressed by fear, and to the citizens of the Empire and every man and woman who wanted order and justice.

As he walked the congested streets of Thénai, rumors reached him of a great sermon the Pontifex preached at the Magisterium, denouncing the lady Lysandra for her abandonment of the gods and her devolution into sorcery. With Black Serpent Lairs in every city, Masimo hoped to the gods that the Pontifex prepared himself properly; but even a ceaseless presence of guards, adamant locks on the doors, and the sacrilege of harming the Empire's holy man, seemed unable to stop the assassins.

The shudder of wood, the shouting on the deck, the thick smell of human habitation, and the faint sounds of the city, proved to Masimo that he was arrived. Half-praying to Animon, half-meditating, he removed himself from the wellspring of magic, temporarily removing all powers of Wind, so that the lady Lysandra would not notice him.

Throughout the bumpy ride along the streets of Korthos, Masimo half-wished he could see the state of things there, and was half-glad that he couldn't. Still, throughout the cart-ride, little glimmers of Korthos' status reached him: the names 'Queen Lysandra' and someone named 'Lord Qabo,' as well as the whispered words 'Dagan' or 'Lord Dagan.'

To calm his nerves, Masimo stayed silent and shut his eyes. He prayed to Animon to give him the clarity and prescience that comes from his high perch on the roof of the world; and in time, the sounds of the city faded away, and there was only the darkness of the barrel.

Masimo stirred awake when his keg was set down. Signor Metellus' voice and the cart-driver had a conversation.

"Give this to Tyros. And take these two denara for yourself."

"Thank you, signore."

Minutes later, Masimo was out in the dank darkness of the cellar. Signor Metellus stood there, his bluish sword of adamant clipped to his belt. Judging by his uncertain eyes, the brave Imperial Knight was seriously on-edge.

"This will be difficult, I fear," he whispered. "She seems to know things before people say them… see things before they come. We must be careful. Without a magic-weaver, I could never defeat her."

Masimo half-opened his mind to the latent magic in the air, and when he did he stifled a gasp. Lady Lysandra gave off a very strong air, and he could tell she tapped the wellspring with amateurish frequency. *An untrained adept, she is…* And the power of the void hung heavy, too, as powerful as the magic itself and perhaps more powerful. She had invited horrible things into her household, though she did not realize it. The madness was probably already setting in. He shut himself off from the wellspring, and gasped for breath.

Signor Metellus was staring at him, and Masimo's anxiety had obviously furthered his own. "It is dinnertime."

Masimo's augur staff leaned against the wall.

"I've told her you're my slave. Your name is Alesso and you're from Gad, and you used to serve a master in Brilium. All right?"

Masimo gulped and nodded, then looked down. *Animon, hold me together.* He felt eyes watching him everywhere, and not human eyes. *Animon help us all.*

~

Entering the Feasting Hall did nothing to cure his nerves. Lady Lysandra, on a raised stone dais, held a jewel-studded chalice in one hand, and a dark wooden staff in the other. A snake in silver thread was embroidered on her pitch-black gown. Her red spicer eyes contrasted sharply with her pale blonde hair. Beside her, a swarthy man with a balding head and an eye patch sat next to her in similar black clothing—her husband, Masimo realized once he counted the fingers, but he had the demure look of a slave.

As Masimo surveyed the rest of the feasting hall, he bit his lip to avoid gasping. To his left, a statue nearly reached the ceiling: six scaly arms on either side, ending in claws; prancing webbed feet; wide crocodilian eyes, and a beard of tentacles. An altar before it had a name, etched in Eloesian script: DAGAN. The altar was stained black.

"Metellus." Even trying to sound welcoming, Lysandra's voice had a caustic edge. "You've returned from your journeying, and with someone else. How are the gutterfolk?"

"The peasants are utterly submissive, Your Worship. They dare not speak anything ill of you or the lord Dagan. I have searched everywhere near Thénai, and have found no more traitors."

"A pity. Dagan hungers. He says nothing satisfied him like the meal he had all those months ago."

"You mean Lucento—"

"Do not say his name! He is dead to me. Now he screams in the Infernal Sea as Dagan's plaything."

The words chilled Masimo like nothing else, and he prayed to Animon that it wasn't true.

"The end is near for us all." Lysandra smiled. "The Last Days are coming. Pick well your allegiance, Metellus. The Great One cometh, and all who worship at his feet will be made lords and ladies in the new world to be made. Pick well your allegiance; I've picked mine."

"You know I already have," Metellus said with an admirable absence of trembling.

"Who is your pet?" Lysandra's smile evaporated. "The great Dagan is unsure of this one. The great Dagan is displeased. Do you see him frown?"

Masimo eyed the demon's likeness and saw no change.

"My domina Lysandra." Metellus knelt and grasped the hilt of his adamant sword. "Alesso means no harm to you, I swear it."

"Then let him kneel at the altar of Dagan. Let Alesso kiss every scale, and curse every god."

Never, Masimo thought. *Not even for this.* "My domina," he managed to say, "I am very tired. The journey from Brilium was long."

An incredulous laugh resounded from the hall. Lysandra's eyes bulged. "The guttertrash dares to speak! He denies the great lord Dagan and insults his vicar. Fall on your face! Prostrate yourself, or I shall lay your heart on the lord Dagan's altar."

That I can do, he thought to himself. He began to kneel.

"Quick!"

He fell prostrate. On the cold stone ground, he half-opened his mind to the wellspring. The void was so strong he could barely breathe; the lady Lysandra had only a glimmer of herself left. Soon the void would try to enter her, to possess her mind; but when unable, it would destroy everything she was, turn her into a mad force of destruction. But, feeling this horrid world she had opened up, he grew cold and breathless. He shut himself off from the wellspring and took deep, steady breaths.

"The lord Dagan does not like this one. The King of the Murky Sea would be much pleased to see him die. He says his heart would be a fitting sacrifice."

"I thought you served the Black Serpent, not a demon," Masimo sputtered.

"*Silence!*" Lysandra screeched. "Do not presume to speak of things you cannot understand. Not even Qabo believed me that the Serpent and Dagan are one and the same; and if even *he* was reluctant to believe, how much more a guttertrash lowblood slave?" She was silent a few moments, but her next words dashed any hope of a changed heart. "Tomorrow evening at dusk, I shall whip you and then flay you. Then the great lord Dagan will have his feast at the shrine in Heaven's Square."

Masimo would have to act soon.

CHAPTER THIRTY-TWO:
THE RETURN

Anthea Adamantus

"Three thousand red cloaks passing by the Arch of Conquest unchallenged." Anthea rarely heard the voice of Edesso, Speaker of the Council, in her personal shrine. "Their ranks have swelled, though I do not know how. Amaraeus' plan is bold. He has made extensive preparations. By any wise estimation, the Redcloaks will be sailing away by sunset."

"I fear the Redcloaks less than Amaraeus." Anthea's grip on the figurine was so viselike it caused her hands to tremble. "Lidda brought our city food and comfort. She has always been kind to me… warm."

"You seem such a devout disciple of the Mother," Edesso said. "Have you heard how Lidda defames her?"

Anthea's grip on the figurine relaxed in an instant. She fell in on herself, body and soul. Tears welled in her eyes. "You are right, Edesso. Ah, Mother. Ah, Melorra… I should not have sent her away."

But the priestess was long-gone down the road. She was probably to the Grand Mother Temple by now, to Amaroth the City of Love. The Revered Sister would treat her better than Anthea had. Why had Anthea reacted that way? Why had she put all those years of friendship aside? Was it so wrong of Melorra not to tell her everything? Was it so wrong of her not to break her heart?

"It feels like I've lost Claudio all over again." In her husband's absence—whom she missed and yearned for with every bit of her mind and heart—Melorra had been her lone friend, her lone companion. *I have lost my only friend, and I have only myself to blame.* "She is gone," she muttered, partly to Edesso and partly to herself. "She is gone…"

She remained in the shrine after Edesso left. She set the figurine in its place; she set the silver likeness of the Mother of all on its stand. One by one she lit the candles of the three Mercies. "Mother protect me. Mother protect us all. But shelter Melorra most of all. Illumine me in what I should do. Show me what is to come. Mother protect us all."

She fell asleep in the shrine, sprawled in the light of the aromatic candles.

A hundred images flashed before her, but most impressionable was a reddish-black mountain in view of a field of purple flowers. Then she was in Imperial City, in the palace itself, and Lidda sat on the White Throne.

Then she was somewhere in Paladium, looking into Claudian's eyes—the son she'd put in a monastery—and, with those beautiful brown eyes holding all the compassion and strength of his father, he said, "Mother, you have abandoned me. Why?"

Then she was in the north, where she'd never been, many years from now, and a troubled wind was blowing through a leaf-scattered autumnal forest.

Then she was in the graveyard, and her body was being carried into the Mausoleum of the Adamanti, and her throat had been cut. She despaired.

But most terribly of all, Claudian's face returned: "Mother, you have abandoned me. You have underestimated me. Why? I have the blood of the god Claudio, and the body of adamant. Why? Why? Why?"

One of the white-winged, luminous Graces, holding a chalice, was there again. "This will all come to pass. But if you overcome, you will rest forever in the palm of the Mother's hand."

After she awoke, she lay there for hours, lacking the strength to stand up.

CHAPTER THIRTY-THREE: THE GODS ON TRIAL

Phido Tribanus

Tribanus' friends around Mud Bottom said he liked the Arena so much, and he spent every aes he got on it, so why shouldn't he be a gladiator. But his friends didn't get it. It was hard to become a gladiator, and it took a lot of training. He'd already missed his opportunity. Twenty-five years was too old to start training. So Tribanus figured that he'd just settle for watching the Arena as a spectator his whole life, and that would be the next best thing.

Tribanus usually loved the competition and how scared he got when he worried the other team would win. When the Sharks of Nichaeus and the Eagles of Imperial City fought in 1048 in a close match, he'd bitten his nails down to the finger, but he loved every second of it. But this upcoming match between the Redcloak prince and Helmur Bloodaxe—between the strange god called "the One" and the gods that everyone else knew and loved—the tension might be even too much for Tribanus to handle. The stakes couldn't be higher, neither. The Redcloaks would leave if Helmur won, and if Helmur lost Tribanus would have to worship the One, and that meant no drinking nor looking at pretty pictures.

Still, he found his gangly legs taking him down the streets, from the slimy huts of Mud Bottom to Imperial Square, where Tribanus never felt like he belonged. A stinker from Mud Bottom, as they called him, had no business in sight of that beautiful palace that the Mud Bottom wisewoman said the gods themselves had carved. He turned down one of the streets. He knew the way by heart, but things seemed different. For one, there were a few Redcloaks around, carrying their weird curved-bladed swords. For another, people seemed quieter, more nervous and less joyful. Tribanus guessed he understood.

Eventually he came to the giant amphitheater. The courtyard just outside, usually wide open, was packed with people. Near the colossal statue of the god Kharn—twenty foot tall, people said, made of bronze, portrayed as nude and wrestling a lion—two men argued and looked about ready to fight.

One was a southron, a Khazidee maybe, short and copper-skinned, and the other was bigger—an Imperial perhaps, but dressed in red to show his allegiance.

"Prince Ashur is going to win, Bashir!" the Imperial snarled. "Anyone with half a mind knows that. You've put all your hope in a redhead barbarian. My father once said, if you can't defeat someone, you should join them."

"Your father died in a gutter, Valentus, penniless and starving!"

The Imperial had turned pink.

"How quickly you turn on the gods. I will never take the Red." The Khazidee's hand had gone to his dagger. "As soon as you hear their threats, you turn yellow. The mother Issa brought floods to Khazan for thousands of y—"

"Quiet, Bashir!" The Imperial clutched a dagger in his trembling hand. "I want to kill you but I cannot do that to my friend…"

The Redcloaks are turning everyone against each other, Tribanus thought, and made his way through the noisy crowd, all the way to the window where the ticket-seller stood. A blonde woman, pudgy and middle-aged, stared back at him. She had the look of an east sider who thought she was better than folk from the Bottom.

"My signora," Tribanus said as properly as he could manage. "I'd want a ticket to see today's fight, please." Every time he tried to talk fancy, he fumbled all over his words.

"We are sold out."

Tribanus' heart sank a bit.

"Except for the private boxes, and those are sixty denara at the least. I don't think you could afford that."

Is it so obvious? But sixty denara was more than Tribanus was like to make in his whole lifetime.

"We do have the standing room for five aesa."

Tribanus dug through his pockets, and counted all he had. Five aesa was everything he owned, everything he was like to get for the next month. But they'd started the free bread again after the famine, and for all the poverty of the Bottom, the people there took care of their own.

He handed the lady the five copper coins. The woman made every effort not to touch his stinky fingers. He took his potsherd, and started for the entrance.

It was noon, and the sun was beating down hot. The folk at the Arena had drawn up its circular awning to protect the audience from the sun. Just about everybody had gotten into their seats. Up in one of the private boxes above him, Tribanus made out the Redcloak woman, the one they called Lidda, with long brown hair and eyes redder than the worst spicer Tribanus ever saw. She was near as pale as Helmur Bloodaxe, but she didn't come from the northlands. The Mud Bottom wisewoman said she came from Hell.

The trumpets pealed. A mounted legionary galloped out of one of the inner gates, waving the gold-red eagle flag of the Empire. Two more followed: a gray-bearded priest of Lorenus waving a white-blue trident flag, and a bald priestess waving the purple ring flag of the mother goddess Amara. Tribanus cheered along with the crowd, and the audience's shouting shook the ground like an earthquake.

Next, from the opposite end, a Redcloak on a sickly gray horse came galloping out from the opposite gate, waving the red-white dragon flag of his own people. There were a few cheers, but much less than the real Imperial-blooded flags.

Once everyone had returned to their gates, the Maestro of Ceremonies walked out from the Imperial gate, wearing a purple-sashed white robe and a thick laurel wreath, and holding a flaming torch. Everyone grew hushed. The maestro shouted so clearly it carried to where Tribanus stood: "Today is a game of life and death! One will die and one will survive! But it is more than that! For whoever wins this game gains something more: the minds and souls of the people! Fighting today are Ashur Dragonstone, Prince of Ascalor, and Helmur Bloodaxe the Barbarian. Ashur fights in the name of the god he calls the One—"

"Blasphemy!" Lidda howled from above.

"—and Helmur Bloodaxe fights in the name of the gods we have revered since ancient times."

"A curse upon the Many!" Lidda howled. Apparently she did not realize how things are in the Arena, that you stay silent when the Maestro speaks.

Unfazed, the Maestro went on: "The game at the Arena today is a trial! On one hand, the gods; on the other, the One! Whoever wins will be worshiped by the Empire forevermore!"

Up in the Imperial Box, the gold-eyed emperor looked pleased. Tribanus wondered why. Tribanus was more frightened than anything else, frightened that he might have to worship a new god, frightened that the temples would all be smashed along with the pretty statues and pictures, frightened that he'd have to give up wine and music and everything that gave the Mud Bottom folk joy.

"Pray to the god you love the best! Without further ado, I call Helmur Bloodaxe and Prince Ashur Dragonstone forward! Let the best god win!"

"Blasphem—" Lidda started but the roar of the crowd drowned her out.

The maestro made a swift exit. The two combatants emerged from either side.

Helmur Bloodaxe was a tower of a man, like all the barbarians were. In both hands, he held a weapon that Tribanus had never seen: a giant double-bitted axe of bluish metal. He was covered in thick steel armor, except for his face—bloodless, red-haired, and blue-eyed—that could not have been more different from Ashur.

Ashur was taller than Helmur, though not by much. In one hand, he gripped a curved saber; the other he let free. Besides steel vambraces and thin gauntlets, Ashur wore no armor except his red cloak. Not only was he taller than Helmur, he was leaner and more muscular. His violet eyes had a commanding, serious air. Tribanus had a hard time imagining that face ever smiling. By Imperial City's estimation, Tribanus would guess Ashur was the more handsome of the two; the ladies would fawn over Ashur far before Helmur, were it not for his severe religion and his inability to smile.

"Today I defend the supremacy of the One." Ashur's powerful, deep voice did not need a shout to carry through the Arena. "I defend the truth that the people of Ascalor have long known. I dedicate this victory to the final defeat of the Many. I dedicate this victory to my lady mother, the Queen of Ascalor, and her ascension to your mortal White Throne."

A few people gasped.

Up in her private box, the woman called Lidda glowed with pride. Perhaps her son Ashur could not smile, but it appeared that she could.

"And I," Helmur seemed at a loss for words, "dedicate this battle to ale and wine, and the frosty winters of the north, and to getting out of this sweltering muck-pit!"

The crowd was silent. Helmur's words were not the inspiring ones they'd hoped for. Tribanus bit his lip. If he had to worship the One, he didn't know what he'd do.

But as Ashur and Helmur circled round each other, the dominant chant was clear: *"Helmur! Helmur! Helmur!"*

It seemed that most everybody in Imperial City felt the same way, that they didn't want the Redcloaks nor the One that they talked about. Tribanus wasn't much of a praying man, nor a real devotee, but he asked the gods in heaven that they'd guide Helmur's axe into the Redcloak prince's chest, not just for their sakes, but for everyone in Imperial City.

Above the chants of *"Helmur! Helmur! Helmur!"* and a fainter chorus of *"Ashur!"* the prince of the Redcloaks darted forward, and the fight began.

CHAPTER THIRTY-FOUR: THE REVERED SISTER

Melorra, Beloved of the Mother

Amaroth, the City of Love. Melorra had not been here in years, or so it seemed. Beyond a thin, shallow channel lay the island-town, centering on the Grand Mother Temple from which it drew its fame. At the feel of the perpetual chilly fog, Melorra wrapped her priestly robe tighter. On the walls of Amaroth, twenty feet tall and circling the island, flags rose above the posts: purple on white, the ring symbol of the Mother. Some said it represented the engagement-ring of marriage, while others said it represented the Mother's infinite compassion; no one knew for certain.

On her white palfrey, Melorra rode through the refreshingly chill air, through the village of Amispont that surrounded the bridge, where—against the wishes of the Revered Sister, but under the instruction of Emperor Claudio—a garrison of Imperial Knights stood guard. The pair of soldiers at the bridge, perhaps at the sight of Melorra's priestly robes and bald head, did not so much as question her.

She had come to Amaroth. The cold fog was as heavy as Melorra ever remembered it: the palm trees, stretching higher than the white buildings; the stone shrines; the hospitals and orphanages; the priestesses, walking by. It was as if they did not know her. But they did.

Some in Amaroth—perhaps even most—believed it was wrong of Melorra to focus on Anthea Adamantus, the preeminent woman in the Empire who did not lack a thing. They did not see the lady Adamantus as Melorra saw her; a woman of wealth and privilege, yes, but a woman with her own struggles, a woman who needed help as much as orphans and widows. Anthea, woman who had sent her away.

Melorra fought the sadness it brought her. The Revered Sister would understand.

And when at last she reached the Grand Mother Temple—a circular building, its domed roof held up by white pillars—she smiled at the thought of seeing the Revered Sister Anorra once again, and she thought for a moment she'd come home.

The hallowed halls of the Grand Mother Temple reminded Melorra of her training, of the teachings of the Three Graces and their Seven Mercies, of her lessons on word-craft to disarm an evildoer by nonviolent means, of studying books on medicine and memorizing each verse from the Book of Love, and of purging all desires for vengeance from her soul.

Amid the pillars, the shrines, the hooded statues of silver, Melorra kept a calm pace as she wound her way through the Mother's seat in the mortal realm. In a room of sickbeds, there was Sister Fiorra, and Diorrus—the only male priest Melorra knew of, who'd endured ceaseless mockery in his hometown for the choice the Mother placed on his heart. Melorra passed them by.

In the courtyard of the circular temple lay a garden full of rosebushes and fruit-bearing trees. Near the center of the courtyard, on a bench, Melorra recognized the lithe shape of the Revered Mother, dressed as she always was in a hooded blue robe. The hems of her dagged sleeves shone gold in the cloudy light. Her shepherd's crook lay lengthwise across her lap.

"Melorra," the Revered Sister said before she saw her. "The world is coming to pieces, and you have arrived on a white horse in the wake. What a blessing to have you here in your Mother's house. I would ask to what I owe the pleasure, but I sense that telling me would bring you pain. And that is the last thing I want for you, sister."

"Revered One." Melorra walked up to her.

The Revered Sister moved her crook out of the way, and Melorra took a seat on the other side of the bench.

"The servants of darkness act more boldly and more openly than they have in remembered time," the Revered Sister said with admirable calm.

"So you have said, in your letters."

"I have looked through the annals of our temple, and I cannot find a single instance of what happened in Korthos. It is an unmatched evil. In the darker parts of our history, sisters have perished at the hands of wicked priests or killed as scapegoats. But never before has an entire sisterhood been massacred, let alone by the government."

"I have been troubled by visions, Revered Sister." Melorra didn't want to bring them up. The thought of the Red Mountain froze her inside. "I am not sure if I have the strength to recount them—"

"Ah, sweet Melorra." The Revered Sister touched her hand. On her index finger was the silver sapphire ring that the Revered wore since the foundation of the order, when the priceless object fell from the heavens. "The bonds of all the sisters and the brother on Amaroth have grown inextricable. We have all seen the vision, and I fear a shadow is falling over the world. It may not happen in our time, or in the next generation's time, but something has been loosed in the world, something impossibly far-away, on a red slope."

"Hush." Melorra had never spoken so rudely to the Revered Sister, but she did not so much as flinch.

"Some priests say the world has neither beginning nor end, only cycles. I am not certain. The Elders of the Far North may know…"

"Do you believe in that legend, in truth? A people beyond the north wind?" Melorra meant to sound incredulous, but as she did she thought to herself that stranger things had come to pass.

"It is said an Elder told us about the Mother…" The Revered Sister abandoned the thought. "We must be vigilant, my sister. I have heard of this Lidda…"

At the name, Melorra shuddered.

"She comes from the land of the r—"

"Hush." Melorra could not help herself. She did not want to picture that evil mountain again.

"Be calm, my sister. I shall not speak of it again, since it troubles you. But be aware, my beloved, that Lidda has more knowledge than we. Your fellow sisters in Imperial City tell me they are uncertain if she opposes the evil that was born on th—" She stayed her tongue. "—the evil that was born in her land. But regardless, the woman Lidda speaks against the gods, even against the Mother of all. When I commune with the Mother she tells me that Lidda is a serpent, a deceiver, a servant of darkness even if she believes that she opposes it. She must be defeated. Perhaps the key is Anthea Adamantus."

The name struck Melorra like the harshest of blows.

"Lidda must be opposed, by violence if need be."

Melorra had never heard the Revered Sister speak so. "The Mother does not smile on violence. *An' the wicked strike you, strike not back and say a blessing unto them.*"

The Revered Sister withdrew her hand. "Ah. Or so it seems. Why have you come back? You were a light in Imperial City, the greatest of the sisters there. You were my ears, my eyes. The Mother's vessel. You pledged yourself in a bond of love, and the ones you bonded to, you have never forsaken."

"She sent me away." Melorra's voice trembled. "But even now I feel her despair. We are intertwined, Anthea and me. Her heart breaks even now. She is weak, even afraid."

"Ah, sister Melorra. Don't you understand? Imperial City needs you. Your beloved has sent you away, but may I repeat the verse you recited to me? *'An' the wicked strike you, strike not back and say a blessing unto them.'* The lady Adamantus has struck you by sending you away. But you have struck her back by leaving her. It should not be so. Imperial City has lost its way, my sister. I have no doubts that if the lady Adamantus sees you once again, she will receive you warmly. She needs you, my sister. And you need her, truthfully."

"I suppose you are right, Revered Sister." Still, Melorra was hesitant. Anthea had been furious. Furious and sad. Still their love-bond remained. It was selfish of her to go this far. The bond told Melorra that Anthea was lonely and afraid. She would ride back to Imperial City through the night. She loved Amaroth and the company of her sisters, but her place was not here.

"But let me be clear to you. Before you return…" The Revered Sister seemed unsure of whether to continue. "In my nightly commune, the Mother has expressed with certainty that Lidda must be opposed at all costs. The consequences of her ascension would be the destruction of the Empire, perhaps Varda itself. Do not use violence; it is against our order. But somehow, Lidda must be removed. Her power grows; like a snake she has wrapped herself around Imperial City, and in time we will be able to do nothing. She hates the gods and the Mother, and do not doubt that she will do the same as Lysandra did in Korthos. If it would further her own goals, she would massacre the Grand Mother Temple and all of Amaroth."

The thought racked Melorra with chills.

"Go swiftly, sister. Do as the Mother wills. Protect Anthea Adamantus your love-bond. And hurry."

On her white palfrey, Melorra galloped out of the gates of Amaroth, across the bridge and through Amispont. The afternoon waxed late. She had not spent a single night in the Grand Mother Temple, and she would be tired at daybreak, but it was for the best. Anthea had sent Melorra away, but she did not know what was best for her. Anthea needed Melorra, just as Melorra needed her.

CHAPTER THIRTY-FIVE: THE FINAL BATTLE

Ashur, Dragonstone Prince of Ascalor

When the rumors of a people who—without dye—had red hair reached Ascalor, it developed and embellished into a legend: a race of men, thousands of miles from the Red Lands, who believed in the One and fought valiantly against the Many. But seeing this pale, flame-haired peasant of a warrior, Ashur began to doubt.

When Helmur got up close to swing his blue axe, his breath reeked of Devil's water, and a true servant of the One would never partake on pain of death. When Ashur ducked Helmur's unskilled, angry swings or somersaulted between his unwieldy legs for show, he'd invoke the Many, shouting obscenities like "Balzor take you!" or "Domnir burn it!"

The battle had gone on several blood-chilling minutes, and not once had their weapons touched. The martial arts of Ascalor were based on speed and skill, not thick armor and cleaving weapons. Ashur could do more with a pointed stick than that unwieldy blue axe. Countless times Ashur had landed a blow, but his saber only grazed the steel plates of Helmur's armor. With each feint and dodge, Ashur eyed Helmur for weaknesses, for openings in the armor, and all he could find was the head—off-limits, people said, in the Arena where the heathens fight. Ashur could have slit his throat a half-dozen times, but the Dragonstone Prince of Ascalor fought by the rules, with honor, so that the One might be glorified.

The dance went on, and Helmur grew more frustrated each moment. His once-white face had turned pink. His obscenities became louder and more vicious. He became sloppier, wilder, and Ashur cut him more often, grazing his armor—and Ashur could have grown frustrated, but unlike these heathens the warriors of Ascalor had patience and discipline.

Another blow of the blue axe, swinging wide. A third, and Ashur ducked. Another, and Ashur dropped to his knees, let it swing by him, and he kicked hard.

The whiteskin barbarian went flying and hit the packed-dirt arena floor. He dropped the blue axe, and it skidded from his grip. It was Ashur's chance. He ran for the blue axe, which would crush the armor if he landed a solid blow.

A pain stung him in his neck. His mind clouded and he began to stagger. *A poison dart.* The heathens had no honor. But they would not prevail. His consciousness faded and returned at random. At some point the whiteskin barbarian was running at him with the blue axe again, preparing to make a final blow. Ashur lifted up his saber and blocked—foolishly, he realized, as the strange blue metal of the axe clove the ages-old Dragonstone Saber in twain.

The heathens were roaring in ecstasy. Another blow came from the adamant axe. *The ancient weapon of Ascalor, ruined.* In a throe of lucidity, Ashur rolled with the blow, let it cut through part of his chest like paper. But it wasn't over yet.

The Kings of Ascalor had treasured the dragonstones—formed in scorching fire of the Red Mountain—above any gold or palace or deep font of water. They had never needed to use them; the ranks of the Deathless had protected them and made such secret weapons unnecessary. Prince Ashur did not have the Great Power, but his mother did. *Surely she knows what to do.*

A half-second before the killing blow would have landed, the black dragonstones—inset on the shattered saber—exploded into a hundred thousand shards. In their wake, a hundred thousand souls burst forward, swirling around in a chorus of blue and white and green. Warped, rotted faces, crying in agony, appeared frequently in the midst of the ghostly light. For a dozen yards around where the black stones had been, the tortured souls long trapped within devoured every soul in their path... every soul except the Dragonstone Prince of Ascalor.

For several seconds they swirled around screaming, and when they had gone on to Judgment, the barbarian Helmur was dead.

In the stunned silence following the victory of the One, Ashur—by now, bleeding heavily—stalked over and grabbed hold of the giant blue axe. He slammed it hard into the soulless corpse of Helmur, piercing straight through the armor and rending open his chest in an explosion of blood and stench.

One wound, one death, one victory, for the lord I serve. Prince Ashur reveled in the heathens' disappointment. He took a bow, and smiled at what was to come.

CHAPTER THIRTY-SIX: THE RED ASCENDANT

Anthea Adamantus

Amaraeus' plan had failed utterly. The Redcloaks and their queen Lidda had taken up quarters in the Imperial Palace, per an agreement the two had made. Anthea did not want to face those crimson eyes of hers, nor her soulless servitors. Again she knelt in the shrine. *It is all at an end,* she thought. And it truly was.

Amaraeus may have thought himself more clever than anyone else in the city, but what reasonable person would stake the faith of the nation on a battle in the Arena? Now the wounded victor Ashur lay in a sickbed in the palace, attended by physicians and his witch mother.

And the religion of our fathers and mothers wil be replaced with the vile heresy of the One. As she clasped the silver figurine to her heart, Anthea wondered if she had been a part of this. Perhaps all the destruction of the temples to come would be her fault. She prayed to the Mother of all that she would not regard her so.

She felt a warm glow before she heard the voice. "My beloved."

Anthea turned. She could think of no more welcome sight than Melorra's blue eyes; and it made her own water. "There is no one I'd rather see. There is nothing else I'd rather see. Thank the Mother! Thank you, Mother!"

Though Melorra smiled, her eyes betrayed sadness, and a hint of fear. "Ah, my beloved. Embrace me, sister."

When Anthea did, Melorra went on.

"The Revered Sister says we must be rid of Lidda. She says it is the Mother's will. Else, the Empire will fall... or become something wholly different from the Empire we know."

"I am not sure which is worse."

"Nor am I." Melorra stepped back. "The path the Mother has chosen is clear. We must be rid of Lidda. We must act with discretion and nonviolence."

Anthea shook her head. "Ah, Melorra, for all your goodness and love for the goddess, you do not understand evil. Sometimes it must be crushed... at the edge of the sword or a poisoned dagger."

Melorra looked down, perhaps afraid to meet her glance, perhaps afraid to show her doubts about restraint and nonviolence.

"The Mother sent me a vision. I will die. I hope it was just a dream. But—"

"No," Melorra gasped. "No. It cannot be!"

There was a shadow in the door. Edesso Vitellus stood there with uncertain eyes. "Anthea Adamantus, my domina." He inclined his head. "Sister Melorra. Lidda requests your presence at her son's bedside."

Melorra's eyes met hers, glazed with the same fear she felt. "Very well." Anthea Adamantus took the lead, trying to remain calm. Still, gooseflesh spread over her skin as she left the shrine. She set the figurine down on the floor.

Lidda's son, Ashur, lay on the bed covered in sweat. He wore no shirt, nothing except a pair of breeches and there—across his once-healthy, muscular chest, a huge gash in his side held the telltale blackish-green color of corruption.

Lidda peered down at him, stroking his arm gently. His short yet thick dark hair and somber violet eyes, his stern nose and noble features, would have made him popular in Imperial City, Anthea thought. *If he did not have a wicked religion, and a witch for a mother, perhaps...*

"Oh, my," Anthea said. "He does not look well."

"The physician said he was poisoned." The lack of emotion in Lidda's voice seemed odd to Anthea, even for a witch. "They say the corruption is spreading fast. He has no chance to live. What do you think, healer?" Her devilish crimson eyes looked up at Melorra.

"I fear I agree, Lidda." Melorra met the witch's gaze only a moment before looking back down.

"Then he will die in the service of the One. A fitting end." When Anthea looked up, those red eyes were boring into hers. "He has… fits… of sanity. He tells me the fight was rigged against him. He claims they injected him with some sort of poison to slow him down. But the One prevailed. Do you believe in the One, Anthea Adamantus?"

"I… N—erm, yes."

A faint smile touched Lidda's lips. "A confession of faith that would please the prophet Joffa."

Irony was often lost on southrons, but it seemed the folk of Ascalor had an acerbic wit. The familiar warmth of Lidda's presence put Anthea at ease, and remembering Melorra's warnings she fought it.

Lidda looked back at her son. "Ah, Ashur. Death takes us all, except those who serve the One. A life is never wasted in His service. If the corruption takes my son Ashur, he will rise as one of the Deathless and he shall be stronger than ever before."

Anthea eyed Melorra. The bald priestess' face had paled so much she resembled an egg. She wanted to comfort her, tell her there was nothing to worry about, that Lidda was not the demon Melorra thought she was. Instead, Anthea clasped Melorra's hand. It was slick with sweat. *The poor thing.*

"My lady Anthea, if I may have a moment alone with you…"

Melorra left eagerly and shut the door behind her.

"Anthea Adamantus." Lidda smiled. "I do not know how you feel about the current emperor…"

I despise him, she wanted to stay, but instead remained silent.

"I have good evidence that Amaraeus achieved his post through illegal means. One witness claims he was in contact with a group of assassins, that he murdered the former emperor Valerio."

"I would not be surprised."

"I believe, under your laws—which I have studied quite diligently—this makes his reign invalid... In fact, he must be deposed. Perhaps even executed."

Deposing him, taking away the circlet, was one thing. Anthea wondered if execution was too far. "We will have to see. I am unsure..."

"The witness has agreed to testify before the Council. His name is Bruno Seánus. Perhaps you have heard of him."

"Yes, I have. He is a... friend... of mine."

Lidda smiled, and her warmth again put Anthea at ease. "Whatever happens, we can rest assured that the One shall punish the deceitful. If Amaraeus achieved his position through ill-gotten means, then we only have one recourse. Do you not agree?"

Anthea nodded. "Yes, Lidda. Amaraeus is a bad man. I have always known this. He certainly does not deserve the Imperial Circlet. But executing him may be too far... perhaps you should merely depose him, remove his titles... send him back to the shadows of the court as a freedman."

"Asura, the Lie-Teller, hides in the shadows. And if this Amaraeus is a silver-tongue like everyone says, we should not want him there. It is best to put the Asuras of this world where they can never resurface. A quick end is best for Amaraeus, I should think."

"Yes, maybe. Perhaps..." Anthea still wasn't sure, neither of Amaraeus' fate nor of Lidda's intentions.

"Your council convenes tomorrow morning. I hope I will see you there." Lidda touched her hand and smiled. Despite her red eyes, Anthea returned it. "I hope we can be friends, my sweet."

"Yes, I would like that." Anthea realized, not without regret, that she spoke the truth.

"I hope that someday soon, you will spurn the Many and dedicate your life to the One."

The words unraveled her. She bit her lip to prevent herself from staggering. "I should probably get some rest, Lidda.

"Of course. I will look forward to seeing you come morning, my sweet."

Anthea turned and left. The air felt much colder than she remembered. Her heart beat quickly, perhaps at all the talk of the One, but she couldn't bring herself to despise Lidda, nor fear her like Melorra.

In the women's apartments, halfway to her bedchamber, a commotion blocked Anthea's path. The former empress Issadore—a gold-haired eastern beauty—held the hand of one of her lovers, a rough legionary by the looks of him, scarred and not especially handsome, but whose presence was less scandalous now that Valerio had passed on. A Redcloak had stopped them, hand on the hilt of a curved saber, shouting at them.

"The palace is now a house of the One, and you defile it. I demand you leave, soldier, at once. The One is holy, and he does not smile on this." The timbre of the Redcloak's voice, though male, resembled Lidda's. "Issadore Lucullus, you bring shame on all our names. You will go meditate at once, leave this ruffian behind, and fast until the One forgives."

"*I will not!*" Though Issadore had good reason for anger, she sounded petulant compared to the Redcloak's stern yet calm voice. "I don't care about the One. Hell take the One! Death to the One!"

The Redcloak jerked the saber an inch out of its sheath. Anthea gasped, thinking a fight would take place in the midst of the women's apartments—something unthinkable until now—but then he sheathed the weapon again. "I shall remember your words, Issadore. I hope you enjoy your wicked deed, for the consequences will be dire."

Gods, does he sound like Lidda.

"Shut it!" the legionary growled. The Redcloak walked off, past Anthea without acknowledging her. But Issadore's gray-blue eyes met hers, filled with annoyance.

They should *be filled with fear.*

"I've had just about enough of these reds," Issadore grumbled. "They've turned the palace into a temple. Enjoying oneself is a crime, now."

"Be careful, Issadore." Anthea's voice trembled. "The Redcloaks do not forgive. They are—" She stopped herself. Lidda's eyes and ears were everywhere.

"If they have half a mind they won't bother me. In Isteros, my father would hang any lowblood who so much as spoke to me."

"You are not in the Vale anymore."

Issadore sneered. "Quiet!" she barked, and led her paramour down the hallway.

If this was the last she saw of her, Anthea would not be surprised.

CHAPTER THIRTY-SEVEN: THE CONFRONTATION

Masimo Vorenus, Augur

The sky outside Masimo's dank prison cell was pitch-black when a commotion stirred him from half-slumber. The warden—once snoring—made a startled gasp. Sword kissed sword, and one broke, riven in two. A jingling of keys, and then footsteps. Before he knew it, Signor Metellus stood there, a blue adamant sword in one hand and keys in the other. He'd set Masimo's augur staff against the opposite wall. A few prisoners begged Metellus to open theirs, too. But Masimo's was the only one he opened. Masimo had a mission, a mission he dreaded more with each passing moment. The lady Lysandra had no skill to her magic-weaving, but she had opened herself up to the void, and that alone gave her no small measure of power.

Wordlessly he passed Metellus by. Still, he closed him off to magic's wellspring. He had to hide himself from Lysandra, catch her unawares, make a quick and decisive blow.

He left the dank prison and found himself once again in the House of the Magistrate, not far from the feasting hall. Red-gold tapestries of the Imperial war-eagle hung from the wall, mixed with pictures of satyrs dancing in the wild forestlands of Themuria. It would seem so normal, but even closed off from the wellspring Masimo could sense the effects of Lysandra opening herself to the void.

Like attracts like, and the House of the Magistrate would not recover from this darkness for decades. The people who lived here—the future magistrates of Korthos—would be troubled with nightmares that left them exhausted. Entities from the void would send pots and pans flying. In the middle of the night, dark voices would cry out. When a house was haunted, the dead rarely caused it. Most often, a sorcerer had lived there, calling upon the void, and the darkness remained for many years. The house of Adrion Magnata, an augur that used the void to avenge himself and soon-after gone mad, had not recovered from its haunted voices and apparitions for thirty years, and by then it had been in such bad repair and had such a terrible reputation that no one lived in it since. Here, in the house of Lysandra—despite his lack of connection to the wellspring—Masimo sensed she had invited entities more fearsome than Adrion Magnata ever had. In time the void would consume her. But Masimo would end it right now.

Avoiding the guards as best he could, he made his way through the twisting nest of corridors, trying to find where Lysandra's bedchamber was. But eventually the winds of fortune bore him to his target. Outside, on a massive balcony, Lysandra slept in the chill night air, sprawled on a chair. One white hand gripped her staff; another rubbed a stone fetish of Dagan. Still, Masimo had little doubt she was sleeping. Her husband Qabo was nowhere in sight. It was the best time to act.

He took in the night air and prepared to open himself to the wellspring. The noise of the Korthosi streets many fathoms below faded from his mind. It was now or never. When he opened his eyes again, the power of magic surged through him once again, and he'd never felt anything so exhilarating. Lysandra startled awake and Masimo thrust his hand forward.

Though not all weavers of magic used staves, virtually everyone focused their power through some sort of talisman. Without it, a measure of control was lost. The power became less shapeable, less focused, wilder and less effective. Disrupting the talisman was tricky and dangerous—for if you failed you would likely disrupt your own grip on the Wellspring—but Lysandra's amateur ability made it more viable.

The staff resisted, forming a wall against him, but Masimo

overcame. In the span of a second, the staff splintered, cracked, and burst in half in a throe of blackish-blue sparks. By now, Lysandra Andereon had stood up and staggered backward, cheeks red and eyes wide with incalculable rage. Her staff clattered to the floor in two pieces.

He summoned Wind, and—hearing approaching footsteps—whipped around to nail Qabo with a sharp gust. The swarthy assassin went flying, and in the distance, Signor Metellus came rushing in with his sword of adamant.

When Masimo turned around, Lysandra had already begun to work her theurgy. She had drawn a simmering, quivering portal with her hands—shifting constantly in shape thanks to her broken staff—and through it lay a world of murky green water, and the two yellow eyes of a fish, quickly approaching as it swam toward them.

Again Masimo called up Wind. Signor Metellus—athlete that he was—had already made it to Qabo and stabbed him in the heart. He had turned his focus to Lysandra when it all unfolded.

A jet of black—half-liquid, half-fire—sprayed from Lysandra's portal. When it touched the sword of adamant, it dissolved it to nothing. Only a half-inch of blade and the hilt was left. Through the wavering portal, all one could see was a black mouth and a pair of yellow, dagger-sharp teeth.

She shut the portal and drew in an exhausted breath. "Traitor!" she gasped. "Traitor!"

"The god Claudio despised traitors!" Metellus growled without a trace of the dark lady's fatigue. "But I have a feeling he would betray you… the murderer of his own son."

Metellus drew a steel dagger from his belt, a much-less fearsome blade than the weapon from before. He ran at her.

"Stop!" Masimo called, but he was too late.

Though racked with fatigue, Lady Lysandra again called upon the Wellspring, upon the black void, and her hands whitened even as a glow of shadow surrounded them. Hand met dagger, and all the infernal energy of the abyss that glowed around her hand filled

Metellus.

He stiffened. His skin hardened. His veins bulged even as he paled. Then he fell dead.

"No!" Masimo called out. The lady Lysandra looked at him, totally exhausted. He savored the pathetic fear in her eyes. Then he drew up Wind, as much as he could muster. Lysandra turned to dart for the hallway. But it was too late. Masimo thrust his hands forward; the concentrated wind took her in the chest, and she went flying off the railing of the balcony, screaming as she plummeted all the fathoms down to the dark streets, all the way to her death.

His mission—the quest that Anthea had sent him on—had been accomplished. The witch Lysandra, murderess of her son, was dead. But shadows were approaching, fleeing down the hallway. A dozen silhouettes, soldiers with armor and spears.

When they arrived, they began to cheer.

"She is dead!" one cried.

"The witch is dead!" another bellowed, and hugged his comrade.

"Thank you, windcaller!" one cried out.

But Masimo's heart was racing. A shadow had begun to take shape in one of the corners of the balcony. The void was strong here, and he had to get out. The shadow stood on two feet, but he had scales and gills, and his head was like Dagan with his yellow fishy eyes, his black tongue and tentacle-beard and scaly skin. The Dagan-headed man was cackling.

More things of the void stepped out of the shadows. The sense of darkness lay heavy over him, a pressure in the air he could feel on his skin, a feeling that sent his already-frail heart racing to an irregular rhythm. He remembered the god Claudio's son, Lucento, and how his witch-wife offered the still-beating heart to the dark lord Dagan. Lysandra was dead but the void remained.

Why were the soldiers laughing? Why were they happy? *The madness of the void is taking me.*

"What is wrong, signore?" a soldier called out after him. "You are a hero! You should be happy!"

"Happy?" The word came as a startled gasp. No, he could not be happy. Not in the presence of the void. He had to leave this place. He would not spend a second in these haunted halls. The Dagan-headed man had vanished back into the shadows but Masimo had no doubts he was still here.

It was time to become the Windwalker. He turned toward the darkness beyond the balcony, the great city of Korthos that stretched many miles into the distance. He started running. He leapt and called up the Wind.

He blew the gales back up at himself, and he floated in midair. *I am the Windwalker,* he thought, but the thing that brought him the greatest joy was to be away from the House of the Magistrate and away from the void, away from Dagan. He blew himself toward one of the roofs. Then he began to fall.

I thought I was the Windwalker. He summoned more wind but he was falling, at first slowly but then like a sack, dropping from the high balcony toward the dark, dim-lit streets. The air rushed him by, the air he could not control.

He thought he was the Windwalker, but now he was only falling, falling, falling.

I am not the Windwalker, he thought, *but at least I am far from the void.* He hit the street like anyone else would have, next to Lysandra's broken body, and not even the magic Wellspring nor the powers of Wind could prevent his death.

CHAPTER THIRTY-EIGHT: THE TRIAL

Anthea Adamantus

Against protocol, Anthea watched the trial unfold from the vantage point of the Yellow Seat. Through threats spoken and unspoken, Lidda sat in the White Seat, though Anthea was anything but her mother. Melorra watched timidly in the corner. Amaraeus—the man for whom the meeting had been called—had not shown up. Perhaps it was best that he did not. Despite all her ill feelings, the vitriol with which Lidda spoke against him had changed her. She did not fear or hate Amaraeus as much, and she did not want—as Lidda did—to see him dead.

Edesso Vitellus, Speaker of the Council, left the lectern and allowed Bruno Seánus to speak.

"My fellow Imperials," the Kings Terrace councilor began, "I have much inside information that I had been loath to discuss. But under the protection of the Redcloaks and the honorable Lidda, I will tell all." He paused, as if hesitant to go on. "Amaraeus hired a man named Marcellus. The west siders called him 'the Bregantine,' for that, I am told, is where he came from. Following instructions from Amaraeus, he went to the Ironfist Monastery where he awaited orders. There, he met the honorable Father Catellus, leader of the Militant Order of Kharn. I present him to you, here and now."

Through a side door, the abbot approached. Though old, he had a healthy look to him, and judging by his walk he was hale as a twenty-year-old. The monks of Kharn—as a sign of devotion to their god—strove to perfect their bodies through rigorous training and a perfect diet.

"My dominos and dominas." Father Catellus looked over the men of the Council and then to Anthea and Lidda. "Bruno Seánus speaks truth. Amaraeus coerced me into providing the assassin shelter.

I have no doubts it was Marcellus that killed Valerio Lucullus. But I'm afraid there is more, much more."

Bruno bit his lip. "There is no need, signore."

"I insist." Father Catellus went on. "Marcellus also murdered the Lornodorsi family."

Anthea gasped, along with several others.

"Amaraeus, observing the man's skill, put him to—by his estimation—'better use.' And who hired Marcellus to murder the Lornodorsi family? Why, the answer is quite clear."

"Shut your mouth!" Bruno ran at the abbot, but Catellus grabbed his arm and thrust him into a headlock.

"Bruno Seánus called me here to provide the truth. He did not want the whole truth, though. Just a sliver. Bruno Seánus wanted the Kings Terrace council seat, and he had no compunction against murdering his opponent."

"Lies!" Bruno hissed.

When Catellus threw him out of the headlock, Bruno went crashing to the floor and hit his head on the hard marble. "No innocent man would act so. I have given you the truth, and now I shall ride back to the monastery."

"Wait!" Edesso shouted, but Catellus was leaving the way he had come, and no one dared stop him.

Anthea had gone cold. *The palace is indeed a nest of vipers.* To think that Bruno Seánus had been responsible for the death of the whole family, all to gain a council seat...

But near her, Lidda was positively glowing.

Edesso stormed up to the lectern, as Bruno Seánus backed away. "I make a motion for the arrest of Amaraeus No-Name, and for this sniveling worm before us..."

Every hand went up.

"The motion is passed unanimously," Edesso boomed.

A Redcloak went darting after Bruno Seánus as he fled.

"My fellow councilors," Edesso said, "we shall have to make amends. Another election will be held for Kings Terrace, and I will send a herald to proclaim all that's gone on. I do not think we have anything further on today's agenda, so I move that we leave early today. All for?"

Before a single hand had gone up, Lidda called out, "Wait!"

Edesso gazed at her. "Yes? What is it?"

"I wish to speak before the Council."

Edesso left the lectern to sit in Bruno's place, and Lidda approached in a swirl of crimson.

As Lidda took the stand, Anthea and Melorra exchanged glances. The blue eyes of the Mother's priestess had gone shallow with fear, and even from a distance Anthea knew what she felt: a strong desire to leave, but a firm determination to see what would unfold in the palace.

"Important people." Lidda smiled. "Great men… and great woman… of the Empire…"

The compliment only sickened her.

"I come to propose this. That I, Queen Regnant of Ascalor, sit upon your White Throne."

A few councilors gasped. Anthea withheld one of her own.

"I fled the Red Lands because the Devil was reborn. The Last Days are coming. The One shall overcome the Devil to destroy the Many. Any nation that loves images—which he abhors—or that drinks the Devil's water, or that teems with license or prostitution or anything other than solemn contemplation… any nation like that shall be destroyed when the One returns. We have a choice before us, O great ones of your Empire, between life and destruction, between judgment and reward, between the One and the Many. Choose carefully. If you decide wrongly, it may very well destroy your soul."

Melorra was silent but quite obviously dumbstruck.

"Even now, my fellow soldiers travel your streets, smashing images where they find them, destroying the shops where they sell

Devil's water…"

"That is a criminal offense!" barked Councilor Donello. If there was ever a good time to use his fiery temper, it was now. "You cannot just come here and expect us to change according to your barbaric customs!"

"Silence!" Lidda's shriek sent even Donello back into his seat. "The One has told me that I shall sit as Empress Regnant. It does not matter whether you wish it or not. When the One speaks, the world will obey."

"You will *not* disobey our laws." Edesso stood up. His voice had a caustic edge that Anthea so rarely heard. "You will not be empress unless the Council agrees. And be assured, witch, that not a single man here would endure you as our leader."

"You reason like a child." Lidda sounded calm. Her anger or joy was impossible to predict. "You will be very sorry, Edesso. The One preserves those who abhor images and abstain from Devil's w—"

"*You* are a devil if I've ever seen one!"

"You have made your choice," Lidda said without emotion, and left in a flurry of red.

At her vanishing, Melorra exhaled.

"She must die," Edesso asserted. "Gods forsake Amaraeus' bet. I won't stake our nation's survival on a match in the Arena."

But Lidda had survived this long, and outwitted them before. Defeating her would be easier said than done.

In the privacy of her bedchamber, Anthea—clasping the silver figurine of the Mother—shut her eyes uttered her nightly prayers. When she sensed a presence, she called out Melorra's name, but when she opened them her error dawned on her.

Lidda stood there, towering over Anthea's bed, her crimson gown nearly covering the floor. "What is that you are holding, my sweet?"

"It is just a little likeness. I don't worship it; I only like to hold it when I pray."

"Give it to me." Her tone made no room for argument.

"Why are you here, Lidda?" She clutched the cold silver tighter, so tight that her fingers began to sweat. "Why have you interrupted my prayers?"

"Be silent." Lidda frowned. "A man tried to kill me while I slept. But the One, and all his servants, protect me. The Deathless follow wherever I go. I wonder if you sent him."

"Wha—? Of course not!" And for once it was truth.

"I suspect you lie. But I shall accept your denial regardless. I am most displeased to see that thing in your fingers. The Imperial Palace is now a temple of the One, and here you are…" She reached for the figurine but Anthea jerked it away.

"Get away from me! I will not let you have it."

"I shall ask you once more. Then, I will force it. Ashur?"

Her son, now one of the Deathless, strode in. A red hood darkened his face, but eyes gleamed in the shadow, and like the rest of the Deathless Anthea could see Lidda behind those orbs.

"You will not have it!" Anthea snapped. "You won't!"

But the deathless Ashur pinned her down on the bed and restrained the hand that held the silver. She scratched and bit and clawed, but this new Ashur knew no mortal pain. He forced it out of her hand and the figurine was gone. Ashur and his witch mother left the bedchamber and Anthea was alone. She wept and cursed herself for not seeing what Melorra had. A demon had entered the palace, and Anthea had welcomed her in.

CHAPTER THIRTY-NINE: CROWNED IN BLOOD

Edesso Vitellus, August

"Amaraeus is gone with a large portion of the treasury. Bruno Seánus is in prison as he well deserves." Rain sprinkled against the Council House's high dome. "Yet the Redcloaks remain. They destroy temples as we speak. The legions are tied up on the northern frontier. But we have little time to act. We must destroy Lidda. We must defeat her quickly."

His voice quivered. The assassin he and Donello sent had perished last night. Lidda no doubt had suspicions and the Redcloaks virtually controlled the palace, letting none in and none out without her consent. Even the Council House—connected to the Imperial Palace by a sky bridge—had Redcloaks at the bottom, preventing escape without Lidda's orders.

"What can we do?" said Councilor Galleo Durantus. "Not even Anthea Adamantus is safe. The prince, Ashur, entered her room and stole the—"

"Ashur is dead…" Councilor Tréano's voice died as soon as it began.

"She raised him with sorcery," Edesso answered. "She is a witch, she—"

"A witch, you say!" The cold female voice that spoke was all-too familiar. Gooseflesh spread over Edesso's skin. "Not the Great Power. Magic. Sorcery and daemon-craft. I am afraid you are wrong." When she strode in, dozens and dozens of Redcloaks followed. Their sabers gleamed in the dim indoor light. "Name me empress. I demand it."

Edesso determined not to let fear get the best of him. The Vitelli served the gods throughout their history, and he deserved eternal torment if he denied them and praised this diabolic One.

"Never!" he sneered. "I will never name you empress, witch. To my dying breath, I will fight you and your One."

Judging by the pale complexions of some other councilors, it appeared that the resolve wasn't unanimous. The god Claudio had despised cowardice. Edesso reminded himself of that as the sword-points gleamed.

"I give you another chance. Will you name me empress?" Lidda said calmly, as if she expected a different answer.

"Never," Edesso sneered.

"Wait. Maybe—" Councilor Donello's voice trembled; for once he was not the rampant lion of the Council.

"A last and final chance. What say you?" shouted Lidda.

"Never!" Edesso called out again, fiercer than before.

Others shouted yes, but it seemed Lidda wanted the consent of the Speaker. She would not get it.

"Very well, servants of the Many!" Lidda screeched. "I will be crowned in blood."

The swords went down. The room, the walls, and the very air soon went red. Screams and gurgling filled what once was a house of gentle debate and argument. Blood dripped from the dome and from Edesso's slit neck. He fell, thinking he might be dreaming. All was red. The world was red. *Lidda has won*, he thought. He wished he could have told his wife goodbye.

Anthea Adamantus

Hidden in shadows, Anthea watched the coronation. Redcloaks surrounded the White Throne, and the Imperial Circlet rested on her auburn hair. With her red gown, and redder eyes, it seemed quite plain that a demoness now ruled the Empire. Anthea had already heard what happened in the Council House: a massacre, a bloodbath. It had only happened once before, and never by a foreigner. She clutched the hand of Melorra, standing by her side, which trembled as much as her own. She thanked the Mother that she had sent Anthea's sister back to her. The love-bond had been tested in fire, and it had overcome. They had been apart for a brief time, but Anthea would never send her away. Nor would she ignore Melorra's intuition, sent from the very Mother herself.

The worst is yet to come. But the Mother would guide her. She remembered her dream, of the trouble that approached her even now, and determined that she would rest in the palm of the Mother's hand.

1051

CHAPTER FORTY:
A BITTER CUP

Anthea Adamantus

New Year's had never been so gloomy. When a rider arrived in Malkat-Ur, the former Imperial City, Anthea braced herself for the worst of disappointments. But through the web of spiders and snakes that now haunted the Imperial Palace, the letter eventually passed into Melorra's hands, and accordingly Anthea. She broke the seal—a laurel-wreath, the symbol of Eloesus—unraveled it, and read:

To the divine Anthea Adamantus,

Lysandra has fallen to her death from the Sky Porch. The demon-shrines have been demolished. Your grandchildren are now in good care, and will be returned to you in the spring. The augur and the knight Signor Metellus have died. But your son has been avenged.

Signed,

Cleon Aryas, Grandmaster of the Imperial Cult

She clutched the letter to her heart. She could not rejoice at the ending of a human life, not even Lysandra's. The demon-shrines were gone, and her grandchildren were safe. But her son was forever gone, and with him, a part of her. She would never be the same.

The Imperial Cult had served them so very well. Anthea hated the fact that the easterners and the southrons considered her divine, but the grandmaster in Imperiopoli had done so much for their family. They were the advocates and the agents of the Adamanti. Without the Imperial Cult—without their network of devotees and spies throughout the eastern world, among them Metellus—this would not have been possible.

Clutching the letter to her breast, she thanked the Mother. *I rejoice not for Lysandra's death, but for justice and for the people of Korthos.* Vengeance was not the Mother's. There were other gods for that.

Morning meant the council would convene. A stab of pain struck her when she remembered there was no Imperial Council anymore. There was only one rule of law, and that was Empress Lidda's word.

She rarely left her bedchamber, but as she stared out on the balcony and saw messengers—bearing the red-gold war eagle standards—she could not help herself. News from the wider world gave her relief from the Imperial Palace that now served as her prison.

When the messengers arrived in the White Chamber, Empress Lidda rose from the throne.

"My domina, news of Amaraeus."

"Where is the demon?"

"He tried to go through the Gate of Tidus, to seek shelter in the northlands. But those gold eyes can't be hidden. The legion has him in prison and awaits your... command." The messenger sounded hesitant to give her such deference. No one wanted to, but the Redcloak army had swelled greatly since her ascension, and besides, the northern legions had never been so hard-pressed in remembered time. The barbarians poured forth like armies of hell. But in truth, Anthea would rather call a smelly barbarian her lord emperor than Lidda.

"Execute him," Lidda said. "He deserves nothing more."

And you deserve far less. Lidda's eyes met hers. Often Anthea wondered if the witch could read her mind. She wouldn't be surprised; she had the whole palace court on puppet-strings and sniffed a conspiracy before anyone said a word. All their best efforts to be rid of her had been thwarted and turned back against them. Melorra told Anthea to wait.

It was hard to wait, though, when the Redcloaks ransacked temples and hoarded the reliquaries of saints, melting them down for the gold. Anthea heard whispered news of silent resistance in the city, of good citizens hiding temple treasures and priests leading conspiracies. Melorra—and Anthea, too—worried for her sisters in Amaroth and the Grand Mother Temple. A garrison of knights protected them, yes, and as a whole Lidda had not yet gained control of the military. Gaining power over the small Imperial Court was one thing. But the legates and even the common legionaries did not fully support Lidda, even if they would not strike her. Above all they respected the Adamanti, but the Adamanti were all dead.

Not all, she remembered. *I am a terrible mother.* Claudian Adamantus, firstborn son, heir to his father, lived in a monastery as far as she knew. Would the legates respect an absent-minded man if he was an Adamantus? It seemed unlikely. But he was her son, and he should be here with her. It was her own fault that he was not. *May the Mother have mercy on my dark heart.*

Lidda was staring at her again. Her eyes were full of thought, always calculating, always estimating. "Leave me," she told the messengers, but her eyes kept focused on Anthea.

Once they were gone, she spoke again.

"Does it surprise you that your people refuse to worship the One?"

"No. We have always worshiped the gods." She'd gone cold. "The Many," she added after a moment's hesitation.

"I think I know why not. My fellow sojourners in the palace tell me that—in the faraway regions of the Empire—some worship you as a living goddess. It is the ultimate blasphemy. Only in Fharas have I heard of such wickedness, and then only in distant times… before your arrogant husband destroyed and reshaped the Southern World."

"Do not speak of him so!" Anthea snapped. She wanted to strike her. "My husband was a great leader and a brilliant general."

"And a wicked heathen."

"I request your permission to leave."

"I deny it." She smiled, perhaps at Anthea's frustration. "In all these months, I have not spoken my mind. It has given me great frustration to see you neglect to honor the One. I suspect that you secretly hold fast to the Many. I have been empress for months, and still the palace is filled with heathens. And I suspect it is all to do with that diabolical woman Melorra. She spreads her deceit and lies. Her love is false. She is a schemer, a serpent, a snake."

"Her love is not false," Anthea said calmly. "But even if it was, at least she shows love."

Lidda laughed. Her reactions were so unpredictable, and that made speaking with her a torture. "*Love to those who deserve it / Respect to those who earn it. / Faith to the One that is mighty.* So saith the prophet Joffa. If I am unkind, your ladyship, it is only because so many in the palace are unworthy." She turned to a Redcloak standing beside her, and snarled, "Fetch me the she-devil."

A Redcloak dragged Melorra into the White Chamber. The ordeal of captivity had turned the once-healthy love priestess pale and gaunt. Her skin clung tight to the bones beneath, and though the Mother's love remained in her blue eyes they no longer had the fire and passion of old. She faced Empress Lidda with a detached, emotionless gaze. She did not bow.

"What are you doing, she-devil? Fall prostrate at once. I will not abide disrespect."

Melorra knelt on the floor. "This is as far as I will go."

The Redcloak captor's boot slammed her down into the proper position.

"Wicked heathen priestess," Lidda said. "I demand that you forsake your dark gods and goddesses, and immediately dedicate your life into the One's service."

"Stop this at once!" Anthea hissed.

Lidda looked up, pink-cheeked. "Silence, blasphemer!" she screamed. Her red eyes flicked back to the prostrate Melorra. "I give you yet another chance. Obey the One and you shall get food."

"You haven't been feeding her?" Anthea half-gasped, half-spoke. *No wonder she is so thin.*

"You shall speak when spoken to, heathen," Lidda snapped. "I ask you again, wicked Melorra. Will you serve the One with steadfastness and an upright heart, or will you continue to starve? You shall be beaten tonight if you give the wrong answer. And I know full well what a weakling you are. You dare not strike back. You are a coward. You fear the One, even though you deny him."

"She fears you!" Anthea shouted. "And for good reason. You are a monster!"

They exchanged glances, and revulsion pulsed through her as she peered into those crimson eyes. "Take her to a cell. We will not feed her, either, until she devotes herself to the One."

A Redcloak stalked toward her. "No!" Anthea cried. She turned and ran straight into another Redcloak's chest.

In the dark, wet prison cell, Anthea huddled in a corner and shivered. Anyone who would treat an old woman like this deserved eternal torment. If what Lidda said was true—and she knew for certain it was false—the world was by nature evil, under the control of a dark god and his servant. But the Mother illumines all, she told herself. She shut her eyes and opened her heart to the great goddess. She whispered, and thoughts entered her mind, thoughts that were not her own.

She has me locked in a cell. I know what I must do.

Melorra was speaking to her; their bond of love was strong, but Anthea did not have her level of power. She could not speak in return.

Stay strong and vigilant, my beloved. Face whatever comes with the Mother's strength. Her Three Graces watch over you. Her power is in you. She is with you until the end of all things.

Anthea's eyes watered.

Your husband's spirit is with you even now.

At the thought the tears began to fall.

You have the strength of adamant. You must be strong. A bitter draught has been poured in the Mother's cup, and you must drink it. But know, my beloved, that it must come to pass.

Anthea wept. She knew just what Melorra meant. Flickers of the dark dream came back to her. The time of her death neared. She wondered if she could face it. She wondered if she had the strength to leave this world with composure and strength. She wondered…

Lay your fears on the Mother. The Three Graces and their Seven Mercies shall stand guard. Even when you are alone, you are not alone.

Anthea rubbed her frail arms together, trying her best to keep warm. She had faced much. Her husband Claudio had conquered everything, brought the world to his feet, and he had died in peace. It seemed unfair. But life is never fair.

Words filled her mind, and she could not tell whether it was Melorra, a remembrance of her dream, or both: *This will all come to pass. But if you overcome, you will rest forever in the palm of the Mother's hand.*

CHAPTER FORTY-ONE:
THE FRONTIER

Amaraeus No-Name

Amaraeus had never seen snow before, except from a distance on the peaks of the Goldenhorns. Now a layer of white crunched underneath his feet when he walked, and he shivered like he never had before. Every day—carefully watched by the Gate Legion—he went for a short walk. He had tried to run twice. The first time, they caught him and threw him back into his cell. The second time, they caught him and beat him until he cried. Amaraeus never cried.

But here he was, outside, on the Empire's northernmost frontier. He wondered how any sane person could live in a place this cold. Traffic had dwindled greatly since the summer, no doubt, but people still passed through the giant gate, a few dozen each day, heading for the northlands.

The icy cold would be his coffin; the leafless oaks and maples his tokens of remembrance. The frontier would be his graveyard.

A messenger rode in, bursting from an icy forest. Perhaps, a message from the witch Lidda, a demand that Amaraeus No-Name be executed.

I was once a man of a thousand faces. I was once everything to all people, but now I am just a man condemned to die.

The messenger was coming from the east, and surely a message from the witch-empress would go directly north. *Then again, she is mad.*

He was from the Gate Legion. Amaraeus had seen him before. He could never forget that pug nose or those facial scars. Falimer, the Paladian. Or was his name Uther? It did not matter.

Junias, the legate, went outside through a door, leaving the doubtlessly-warmer quarters.

This has to be important.

"My domino!" the Paladian shouted.

Junias wanted everyone to call him 'domino,' whether slave or free. It came easy to Amaraeus.

"The Border Legion is in chaos. They have no man to spare."

"The Ninth Paladian says they won't help if the Thirteenth Bregantine comes, and the Thirteenth says the same." The messenger shrunk under Junias' glare.

"And?" Junias's anger was palpable.

"I went to ask the Thirteenth for their help, but they had already left. Apparently the Ninth Paladian and the Thirteenth Bregantine are battling right now. So…"

"So we have no one," Junias intoned. "These pathetic squabbles would have never happened ten years ago."

"Claudio is gone," the messenger said.

"Really? I had no idea," Junias growled, his tone dripping with sarcasm. "Get your sword and shield, Falimer."

I was right the first time.

"Wulfrik is coming, and we face him alone."

The war chief himself. He has probably already crossed the River Gad.

Junias was glaring at Amaraeus, now. "Get inside, Gold-Eyes. You've got a short break today. We've got more important things to worry about than you."

"Then let me g—" A hard shove from his guardian stopped Amaraeus' suggestion. In sight of the stalwart maples he walked, across the white snow of the north, back to his dank dark cell. But at least it was warm.

At night, the drums began to pound. *Boom, thrum-thrum-thrum, boom.*

A low horn bellowed, and Amaraeus sat up in his stone-walled cell with a gasp. Perhaps the goddess Issa had rewarded him for his patronage. Perhaps this was for the best. This could provide a distraction. Or perhaps, somehow, he could communicate with the war chief.

Boom, thrum-thrum-thrum.

Yes, perhaps he could use this disaster to his advantage.

Boom.

The legion began to chant, and their own drummers started playing. Trumpets pealed. The *clack* of ladders striking the wall soothed Amaraeus. Perhaps it was the cold, or the walls surrounding him, but despite all the noise and the panic of the soldiers above, he found himself drifting asleep.

The door opened, and Amaraeus gasped. Falimer stood there, bleeding from a huge gash on his arm. "Come with me, Gold-Eyes! There is no time."

The moustached Paladian turned and ran, and Amaraeus followed him.

Despite the darkness of the night, it was clear the barbarians had overcome the legion. They now poured down from the Wall, looking like huge beasts in contrast to the Imperials.

They would ravage the nation now, steal everything valuable and burn everything that wasn't. A few hundred yards outside the gate, Falimer fell to his knees and gasped for air.

Amaraeus' own heart was racing, but he did not want to stop. "Come on. We need to—"

He turned back. The barbarians were grinding open the Gate of Tidus. Others poured out.

"Junias is bleeding up there, probably dead by now. Not even the gods could save him, now." The snow around Falimer had turned red. "It's probably near morning now. It's—" He burst into a fit of coughing.

A shadow was approaching: horn-helmeted, no less than six feet tall, and a battle-axe in hand.

"Junias told me to take you to Imperial City, but…"

Amaraeus sprinted away before Falimer could finish. When he looked back, an axe had taken the Paladian in the back of the skull. The sight sent fire through Amaraeus' veins, pushing him to sprint faster, pushing him to bolt southward into the snowy frontier lands. How far to Brilium, he wondered, the northernmost town? But even that wouldn't stand against the barbarians. Not even Bregantium could. The barbarians destroyed everything; man-for-man, they were better fighters. Only the Wall that the ancients built stopped them. Only the Wall prevented the Empire's total destruction.

At times like these, he needed a horse.

Hooves pounded against the earth. Amaraeus looked back. A horse was coming, but not like he wanted. The rider wore the horned helmet of a barbarian, held an axe the size of a chariot-wheel, and he let out a crazed scream that only a berserker could make. Amaraeus ran as fast as he could, faster than he ever remembered running in his life.

"Domnir! Domnir!" the berserker screamed. "I give this man's blood to you!"

Amaraeus ran even faster, heart exploding out of control, blood ice-thin with panic, chest heaving with breath. He prayed to Issa, but the goddess' name had barely left his lips when the steel axe opened his body, crushing his ribs and spine as it sliced through him like butter.

CHAPTER FORTY-TWO: THE BODY OF ADAMANT

Daimon Hierastos, Malleus

Daimon was seven days past the Bridge of Pallister, warhammer strapped to his back, and his journey was near over. No one dared bother him, as long as he wore the paladin surcoat and professed his faith to Hieronus. Of course, he did serve the god of justice, but he served another god as well. A god that—to the detriment of the people of the Empire—had died. And it was that god, Claudio-Valens Adamantus, that brought him to Sanctum.

By law, a paladin could not belong to the Imperial Cult. But if the Pontifex knew Daimon was involved, he made no effort to stop him. Besides, even if Claudio was not the god whom Grandmaster Cleon claimed, the mission had serious bearings on the good of the nation, both from within and from without.

But in truth, Claudio-Valens *was* a god—if not by Heaven's reckoning, then by man's—and Daimon Hierastos was unworthy to worship at his feet. Grandmaster Cleon had convinced Daimon of that, as had reading of Claudio's life, of how he had succeeded in every venture and subdued the world, as if the very fabric of Varda bent at his command.

It was Daimon's holy duty as a paladin to—in Grandmaster Cleon's words—go to the holy city of Sanctum and reclaim the "godsblood" for the good of the Empire.

The stench of Sanctum grew in Daimon's nose, and when it built to a pinnacle the white-walled city appeared before him, gleaming in the sun.

At Eagle's Gate, a pair of white-garbed Templars—most senior of the paladin order, whose faith supposedly manifested in displays of divine power—allowed him to pass with silent, derisive nods.

Then he arrived in Sanctum, filled with monks in gray habits and vestals in white hoods. Daimon had trained here, in the faith of Hieronus and in the art of combat. He could count the taverns on one hand, and none of them tolerated drunkenness. There were no whorehouses that Daimon knew of, though his fellow students had searched for one. There were no gambling houses or spice dens or anything that the Pontifex condemned. But for all its piety and morality, the punishments for transgressors could not be any more severe—a thief lost a hand, a peeping tom an eye, a liar his tongue—and some wondered if that made Sanctum holy after all.

Along the main stretch of road, the only buildings one could see were temples and the only people one could see were priests, paladins and the occasional Templar. Some might think the people fed on the goodwill of the gods and drank holy water. It was difficult to find a grocer's market or a bookseller or a smithy, but if you tried long enough they could be found.

The Saint Traber Monastery lay in the shadow of the Magisterium, a humble building in comparison to the great works of architecture that filled Sanctum. There were plain windows rather than stained-glass; a tile roof of faded red; a plain stone edifice without masonry. But it was here, in this humble abode, that the godsblood resided.

Daimon entered without knocking.

The abbot greeted him in the vestibule. "My good Signor Malleus." The lean man had his hair cut in a tonsure. If it weren't for his wrinkled hands, Daimon would have thought him young. He moved with the alacrity of an athlete, and in his gray eyes was the fire of youth. "How may I assist you?"

"I come for the godsblood," Daimon said firmly. "I come for Claudian Adamantus."

The abbot went pale.

When the godsblood walked through the door, he wore the same brown habit as the abbot. Daimon knew through careful study that the son of Claudio was forty-one years old, but—like his liege the abbot, perhaps through exercise and careful regimen—he looked no older than twenty.

"Claudian." Daimon fell to his knees. "The blood of the god runs in your veins. Your Empire needs you. You must take up a sword and claim your birthright, the world."

Claudian's brown eyes looked unsure. "M-M-My b-birthright?"

What was a stutter to a god? "The world is your birthright, O godsblood. The very universe is your birthright. The grandmaster knows this, and so do I, even if you do not."

"I did not think you were part of the cult," the abbot said, sounding unfazed. "I shall not tell anyone. The Pontifex does not need to know."

"Now you do." Daimon spared a second's glance at the abbot, then returned to the godsblood's timid eyes. "Take up your sword. The legions will follow you. You are the son of the god. You will be treated as a god. Take up your sword and your devotees will follow."

"I n-need n-no s-s-sword of s-s-steel. I h-have a m-mind of s-steel, a-and the b-body of a-a-adamant."

"Indeed you do," Daimon said.

"It is the credo of our order," the abbot said, "The Monks Militant of the Order of Saint Traber."

"By your godsblood, you will conquer," Daimon said. Slowly, he rose. He felt unworthy in the presence of a divine. "By your godsblood, and by the body of adamant, you will take your birthright."

"B-by t-the b-b-b-body of a-a-adamant I w-will c-conquer."

Claudian's eyes retained their timidity. Daimon would teach him what he was, the blood of the god. "B-by the b-body of a-a-adamant, and b-by t-the g-g-god's b-blood."

And indeed he was. Whether a stutterer or a fool, Claudian was the godsblood, and with Daimon's help he would—like his father before him—claim the very world.

CHAPTER FORTY-THREE:
A FINAL TASK

Melorra, Beloved of the Mother

Help is coming, the Mother told Melorra. But it would not come fast enough. She had gone from a priestess of the goddess to a common servant. Exhausted, she scrubbed the caked-on crust off a pot as two scullions washed the floor around her. The lady Lidda ate her noontime meal right now, and none of them would eat until the kitchen sparkled with cleanliness. Of course, Melorra would only get scraps from the lady's plate. The other scullions—two Anthanian boys, once attendants of Anthea—had professed their faith in the One, and in return Lidda treated them humanely.

Melorra would never do that.

Other slaves had already served the spicy lamprey stew, but the kitchen still felt like a boiling pot. Sweat slicked every inch of Melorra's skin. She thought she might faint, but the Mother gave her strength. Anthea was far worse off. Lidda refused to feed her until she submitted to the One. But Anthea was strong as Melorra hoped she would be. She had refused, and Melorra had tried her hardest to feed her. But Lidda had placed Redcloaks in the cell, and she could not change the Redcloaks' hearts, like she had changed Lysandra's servant Leonas. The Redcloaks' eyes were Lidda's eyes, and the Redcloaks' hearts were Lidda's heart; and Lidda had gone too far into darkness, too far into shadow, to see the Mother's face.

"Melorra."

She gasped and looked back. A Redcloak stood at the kitchen door.

"Empress Lidda wishes to speak to you."

The White Chamber had never seemed so gloomy. Now, a

woman in red sat on the enormous White Throne. Her bowl of stew had been licked clean, from all appearances. But she looked hungry. Not hungry for food, but for violence.

"The heathen priestess has come," Lidda laughed. "I fear she will regret obeying me."

Lidda rose from her seat and walked toward Melorra, across the polished marble.

"You have a choice, Melorra, and power over you and your friend."

"I have no power except by the Mother."

"Silence, blasphemer!" Lidda clawed her in the face.

Tears of pain filled Melorra's eyes. She touched the flaring wound and her hand came back red.

Lidda was smiling now, positively radiant. "Ah, I like having you here, Melorra. I can do whatever I like to you, and you won't resist. You are the very definition of a weakling, and in Ascalor we like to keep the weaklings for show. However, we punish brazen idolaters severely. I shall not be so kind to your friend. I shall kill her, unless you save her."

"No! Do not kill her!" Melorra wept. "She is my beloved. Do not harm her, Lady Lidda, I implore you…"

"Silence!" Lidda screamed. "You may help her, Melorra. She refuses to honor the One. Like all the children of the Many, she loves images and Devil's water. My son Ashur had to pry that silver idol from her hands."

Melorra's salty tears stung her cheek wound. She had given the figurine to Anthea as a gift. It was only silver, but often the unpracticed daughters of the Mother needed something tangible, something physical, to pray.

"If you confess your faith in the One, heathen priestess, then I will not kill Anthea Adamantus. If you hold fast to your idolatrous goddess, then she shall be executed at sundown."

"Lady Lidda, you have put an awful choice before me," Melorra said. "To choose between my heavenly Mother and my earthly sister? Is such wickedness common in Ascalor?"

"Wickedness?" Lidda bellowed. She clawed her again, from the other side, and it hurt more than the first time. Then she kicked Melorra, sending her to the floor. Melorra lost her breath, and Lidda cackled. "So it is your choice. You have betrayed your friend."

I have betrayed no one, Melorra thought. *My beloved would want this. My beloved would rather die than see me honor your devilish One.* Melorra said nothing, guarding her tongue. She had to bite her lip to prevent herself from speaking. All her life and energy had gone from her, but she had to be shrewd. Everything hinged on Melorra, everything that mattered. That is what the Mother said.

"For your unrepentant blasphemy, you deserve fire." Lidda smiled as Melorra struggled to breathe. "In times before the true teachings of the One, the heathens that lived in Ascalor tossed newborn babes in the fire to gain the favor of the Devil. That is the fate you deserve, wicked creature. Before we knew the One had another side to himself, that is what the Ascalori did. And when the unrepentant refused to listen to the prophet Joffa, the good servants of the One bound those Devil-worshippers to pyres and burned them on Mount Tophet."

And how is that better than before? Again, Melorra kept quiet. "And that is what I deserve, you say."

"It is," Lidda answered. "You deserve a burning. But instead I shall make you miserable, Melorra, until you can no longer bear it. Then you will honor the One. And I know that you cannot fight back, according to your vows with the Many. Eventually you shall wish for your death. But it shall not come. It shall not come until you put aside your wicked goddess and honor the One."

"And if I do not?"

"You will." Lidda smiled. "Soon, the yoke I have placed on your neck will be too much for even a priestess to bear. And you will join the rest of those still alive in the 'Imperial' court, and honor the name of the One. That will be a great day. But tonight, at sundown, there will be only death. Anthea Adamantus shall answer for her clouded judgment, her wicked devotion to her wicked goddess, and then the people of Malkat-Ur will know the truth."

The truth, that you are a demon. Except in Lidda's presence, Melorra refused to call Imperial City Malkat-Ur. "I beg you to reconsider, Your W—Your Honor." Even now Melorra could not bear to honor her with Imperial title.

She noticed. "I want you to scrub the whole White Chamber clean, heathen. Then I shall likely dirty it again, while you are scrubbing my bedchamber."

Melorra looked into those crimson spicer eyes for only half a second before she could bear them no longer. In time she got to work.

It was late afternoon when she finished cleaning the White Chamber. She only had a little time left. There was only an hour to spare, if that, and there was one last task before her. Melorra's heart felt heavy as lead, and though her tears had dried she felt like weeping. Quietly as she could, she headed to Lidda's bedchamber to clean it. To embark on the task her mistress had given her... and another.

CHAPTER FORTY-FOUR:
THE PALM OF THE MOTHER'S HAND

Anthea Adamantus

Today, the scullion that brought water to her cell told her what had happened to Issadore Lucullus. Lidda had shaved her head like one of the priestesses, denounced her in front of the people, and then executed her by sword-blow in Imperial Square. Issadore had made poor decisions, dark-hearted ones perhaps, but the punishment did not fit her error, and the ire and hatred of Lidda exonerated Issadore of all her mistakes. Now, Anthea loved that loose Eloesian blueblood more than she ever had. And her time was coming.

The scullion told her Lidda meant to execute her. Anthea would not give the witch the pleasure of seeing her weep. She would not beg the witch for her life. She would face what came with strength and resolve. She would trust and she would die like a proper empress, her attitude as noble as her station.

When Lidda's red eyes met hers, Anthea did not look down. She faced them and rose, weak and light-headed from hunger. Despite her dizziness and rags of clothing, she would face it all like she should. *Like an empress, in the palm of the Mother's hand.*

In the White Chamber, Melorra waited for her in her azure priestly gown. Her eyes were shallow, her face white and egg-like, her lips colorless. She looked gaunt, bone-thin, and weak, more wretched than she'd ever looked, but Anthea had no doubts that she herself looked worse.

"Here is the one that sent you to her death," Lidda said from behind, and Anthea could hear her wolfish smile. "She has converted to the religion of the One, and has forsaken you."

Melorra wanted to say something, but she eyed the Redcloaks

in her chamber with their sabers and did not. "You heard her," she exhaled. "I have forsaken you."

Anthea stifled a breath. When she fell, her old knobby knees burned like fire. *My only friend has betrayed me… the world will honor the One. There are no gods. There is only darkness.*

"Get up!" Lidda howled.

Not a trace of compassion in her voice. Anthea stood up and her knees burned worse than they ever had. The pain broke her tears free, the tears she had meant to never shed.

"You shall pay for your disobedience." Lidda snarled from behind.

"A last embrace, for the friendship I forsook." Lidda's growled objection could not prevent Melorra from running to Anthea.

Anthea tried to resist, but Melorra overcame her, and the cold of metal touched her hand. She looked down and found the silver figurine she had lost in the palm of her hand.

The palace overlooked Imperial Square. Escorted by Lidda, the journey took only a few moments before she reached the crowd. *Ah, yes, a crowd.*

Thousands watched, thousands of faces—men and women, Imperials and southrons, god-fearers and Redcloaks—and, almost without exception, frowning. A few angry jeers of "Let her go!" were met with a snarl from Lidda.

Anthea walked on, fingers hiding the silver figurine as best she could, having wiped the tears away. There would be no weakness shown, not even unto death.

Even if her people wanted to rescue her, a living wall of Redcloaks three men deep blocked them off. She'd heard a rumor that most weapons had been confiscated, even though citizens were allowed swords by ancient custom. She had little hope to escape. She would face what came. If the gods existed, the witch Lidda would get what she deserved. On the north edge of Imperial Square, in front of the lectern and the High Podium, was a chopping block.

A Redcloak forced her toward it, as Lidda climbed the podium and headed to the lectern, the place where announcements of the court and news of the wide world had once been proclaimed to the citizens. *What a better time that was.*

She determined to make her husband Claudio proud in his heavenly glory. She determined to honor the memory of her son Lucento. She prayed to the Mother that Claudian would find it in his heart to forgive her, and that he would escape Lidda's wicked wrath. *Ah, Claudian. A monastery was never the place for you. I thought it was best. Gods help me, I thought it was best.*

"A winter's day, cloudy and sunless, is fitting for this one's death-day," Lidda began. "She refuses to honor the One, brazenly denying the truth. She is a child of the Many. I have treated her well."

"She tortured me," Anthea's voice carried, much louder than she expected. "And still I would not forsake our nation and our gods!"

"Lies!" the witch Lidda hissed. "The woman lies! She is Asur'ashan the Lie-Teller embodied."

Anthea determined to speak no more. She stroked the figurine, still in her right hand. She would not keep it hidden forever.

"I have tried so hard to bring her into the truth," Lidda went on. "I have tried so hard to change her and help her see her error."

The Redcloaks were inching her toward the chopping block. Anthea would not struggle against them; they were strong, and she was an old woman.

"She clings fast to her vile Many. She still profanes the name of the One. We have a saying in Ascalor: 'Give a man one chance to change his ways. If he refuses, bind him and burn him on Mount Tophet.' Therefore, Anthea Adamantus, you have one chance to change your ways and soften your hard heart. Do you forsake your vile Many? Do you swear your loyalty to the One?"

"Balzor take your One!" Anthea shouted. Invoking the god of death was improper for an empress, but she couldn't help herself. "And let worms feast on his corpse!"

Lidda fell back from the lectern, perhaps stunned. She had lost her breath. A few in the crowd cheered. Another angry "Let her go!" was disobeyed. But finally Lidda fell back to her place at the lectern and hissed, "Off with her head! Now!"

Perhaps Anthea should not have said that, she thought as they forced her head onto the chopping block. Perhaps, perhaps. She should not have done many things. She should not have sent Claudian to a monastery. She should not have held a grudge against her husband, who by anyone's estimation loved her more than Sofia. She should not have accepted the gifts of the Redcloaks, who brought with them spiritual poison. There were so many things she should not have done.

Knees flaring, bent over on the chopping block, she no longer tried to hide the figurine. Had Melorra betrayed her, she wondered. It did not matter. None of it mattered. All that mattered was that she faced her fate with resolve. The cold of the blade touched her neck.

Tears fell unbidden from her eyes. She wished she could see Lidda's downfall. She wished she could hold Claudian once again. She wished, she wished. She should have, she should have.

The crowd was roaring when the first blow fell. Her spine gave in, but as the last glints of life remained she heard their cry: "Deicide! Deicide!"

It was not what she wanted to hear.

Lidda screamed in return: "Kill everyone who resists you, men of the Red!"

Another blow fell. Her eyesight faded. Her grip on the figurine loosened and it fell. The figurine didn't matter. All that mattered was that she did what required. That she faced her life's end. That she faced her death in the palm of the Mother's hand.

CHAPTER FORTY-FIVE: WASHED IN BLOOD

Melorra, Beloved of the Mother

A month had passed since the darkest day of Melorra's life. When the love-bond broke, all joy had left her; a gloom filled her emptiness, a void from which she would never recover. There was no energy anymore, no feelings, nothing. But there was something still to be done. Something for which she had let Anthea die.

News of the wider world had come to Melorra's eavesdropping ears. The barbarians ran free in the north. Bregantium was under siege last she heard, and likely had fallen by now. The Gate of Tidus lay open. And Claudian Adamantus was gone from his monastery where his mother had placed him, with two legions following behind. Some said the man was a fool, but his Adamantine blood overcame it in the eyes of the soldiers.

Even that could not break Melorra's deadness of heart. *Why me,* she asked the Mother as she so often had of late. *You have given me a bitter cup.* But no bitterer than Anthea, her companion and beloved.

The execution had enraged the people, Melorra was certain of that. The resentment still boiled. But the Redcloaks had total control over the city, and the Imperial citizens—though notoriously proud— would be broken like a wild horse in time, if something was not done. At the thought of the Empire revering the One, Melorra shrugged off a stab of despair. She had looked so hard for an opportunity to accomplish what needed to be done—the goal she had, the one the Mother did not approve of, but that she knew in her mortal mind was necessary.

In the White Chamber, she gazed at the red-eyed empress. "Your Undying Glory." The words tasted bitter in her mouth. "I have seen the error of my ways. I wish to forsake all the things I have ever revered, and pledge myself into the service of the One."

A smile spread from one ear to the other. "It shall be done. And tonight we will serve the richest of feasts on your behalf. The timing could not be better. The child of Asur'ashan is mere miles from the city, and he has responded to my messengers with insults and blasphemies. It shall bring me great joy to see him look in your eyes, and see the priestess of the Many profess the One."

Asur'ashan. Lidda did not use the name Anthea. Even now, Lidda could not get over her insolence. Anthea's death had not taken away her burning wrath. Lidda still remembered how she had resisted her to the very end, how she had died with a blasphemous insult on her lips. Sometimes, the witch would cry—crocodile tears though they were—or take the bitterness out on a palace slave. Anthea had an effect on Lidda, even beyond death.

"We must go to temple," Lidda said, for once smiling brightly. "I—the High Priestess—shall sprinkle my blood on you. The blood will represent your change of heart, your journey from falsehood to truth, from the lies of Asura to the power of the One. What a great day this is, Melorra. You have seen the error of your ways. You shall not regret it."

As soon as Lidda faced away from her, Melorra stopped smiling. A cold dread grew in the pit of her stomach.

Lidda had outfitted one of the women's apartments into a small temple. According to Ascalorian custom, no statues or images decorated the room. Bare stone walls, two candelabras, a plain altar, and a red cloth comprised the whole temple; but it was here that the High Priestess of the One conducted her religious duties, where she laid offerings on the altar, and where she swore in new converts.

Converts. The thought of forsaking the Mother caused a half-snarl to cross Melorra's mouth. *But that is why I am here.* That was why she told Lidda she was here.

In a swirl of red Lidda took her place behind the altar. In an instant, a knife was in her hand: a curved Ascalorian weapon, shimmering in the flickering candlelight.

"Praise the One born on the Red Mountain," Lidda spoke. "Praise the One who shall overcome himself, and then overcome the heathens and their Many. Praise the One who fell in ages past, whom the Many smote on the baleful tower, but who shall come again with unstoppable strength! Praise the One who shall rule every world, and remake them all." Her red witch's eyes met Melorra's gaze, gleaming with rapture. "A woman has come to forsake the Many, to sprinkle her blood on your altar." Her voice took on a booming tone. *"Give me your hand, heathen!"*

"Should not I cut my own hand?" Melorra spoke gently. "I, who strayed so long? Who resisted with all I had, but learned to submit?"

No, the Mother cried from Heaven. *No! It is not my way.*

All the trust she had built up, the beatings she had endured without complaint, the absurd commands she had obeyed, the abuses both physical and spoken without vengeance, now rested on this moment. The red eyes looked hesitant a moment. Lidda thought she had nothing to fear.

"Yes," Lidda said. "Yes, yes… it shall be…"

No, the Mother cried, but Melorra ignored her. *It is not my way.*

Melorra had the hilt of the knife in her hand. She put one hand on the altar. She put the cool of the knife-edge across her fingers.

No, the Mother told her, fainter this time. *Do not.*

Melorra looked up into the witch's red eyes, her cold, glaring face bearing no awareness of what was to come. Melorra would not enjoy this, though she knew that many would. This was pure duty… this was…

Can I do this?

"Melorra, child," Lidda began.

She leapt to her feet and attacked.

CHAPTER FORTY-SIX: THE GOD RETURNS

Daimon Hierastos, Malleus

At the Arch of Conquest, the Redcloaks formed a solid wall. They had the advantage of numbers, but the combined Ninth Paladian and the Thirteenth Bregantine Legions had another… a god.

The god Claudian Adamantus walked at the front of the army. He still wore the brown monk's habit. He refused to wear armor like his legionaries, and he wouldn't touch a sword or spear. He claimed, as a Monk Militant of the Priesthood of Hieronus of the Order of Saint Traber, that he had gone beyond the need for mortal arms.

Talk all you want about regimens and exercise and meditation. Daimon knew it was his Adamantine blood, the divinity that passed from father to son.

The Redcloaks stood still like a wall, unmoving with their shields and sabers. Faces peeked out of upper-story apartment windows. Some looked happy; others looked afraid.

There is nothing to fear, Daimon thought to himself. *We shall fear nothing when the god of the Empire marches at the vanguard.*

Claudian stepped forward. "I-I w-wish to sp-speak with your l-l-leader."

A javelin flew at Claudian from behind the Redcloaks, then two more. The first bounced off the paved road and clattered to the floor. The next went straight toward Claudian's chest—Daimon drew an icy breath—but Claudio ducked in, catching it with his right hand, and deflected the other spear before assuming what he called the "scorpion stance."

He would give all the credit to his training at the monastery, but Daimon knew full-well it was his divinity.

Now, it was clear the Redcloaks did not intend to play fair.

"Charge!" Daimon shouted. For all his power, the monk

Claudian said he was a fighter not a general. "For the sake of the godsblood, *charge!*"

The legionaries ran at them, but the battle was already won. Before the lines converged, the Redcloaks were falling dead, left and right, as if their souls were leaving them.

It is not we that have won the battle, Daimon pondered, *but the godsblood. And now he shall sit on the White Throne, and claim the world as his birthright.* A chill ran through him. The glory of his father the god gleamed all around him. By the godsblood, they had won the day. By the godsblood, the Empire would prevail.

CHAPTER FORTY-SEVEN: MIDNIGHT FLIGHT

Melorra, Beloved of the Mother

As she ran, Melorra gave one passing glance to the mangled, slashed-up body of Lidda one last time, dropping the Ascalorian saber from her ever-weakening hands. The dragonstone in her necklace had burst to dust, and a chorus of ghosts swirled everywhere around her, filling the room and the very halls of the palace with their tortured cries.

Her weeping increased as she fled through the palace halls. The lifeless bodies of Redcloaks lay at the posts and chamber doors they guarded, gone from the witch's spell of false life.

She could no longer feel the Mother; their connection had been severed. *How fickle the goddess is. I did my duty, and she will not forgive. She has always told us to forgive.*

She kept running, her only goal to get out of the palace, to get out of "Malkat-Ur"—no, Imperial City—and flee, perhaps to some far-flung northern town and perhaps into the briny sea.

As she ran, the memories of what she had done flashed back to her. Of Lidda begging for her life as Melorra slashed her open again and again. Of the childlike desperation in the witch's eyes—evil though she was—and how Melorra had broken every oath of her sisterhood, how the anger and bloodthirst of the uninitiated returned to her, how she had not only done what she intended to do… how she had enjoyed it.

She cried out at the thought, and nearly fell. But she kept running, running, running to the stables.

And once back on her white palfrey, she galloped away, avoiding the crowds, and rode into the coming night.

Three days out of Imperial City, going ever northward, penniless and sleeping wherever she could find shelter—in alleys or under the rare tree—she found herself on an ocean cliff, looking over the blue waters crashing down on rocks far below. Gulls flew overhead, crying out. The air smelled of summer.

Behind her, purple flowers rolled in the gentle winds, and a cluster of holm oaks broke the monotony of apartment blocks that plagued southern Anthania. As she looked back, eyes welling with tears, she remembered the town of Eximenius lay just a mile away. Such beauty here, such serenity.

She had lost Anthea her love-bond, though by calling the One her lord she could have saved her. But because she had saved the Empire from destruction, from the replacement of all their gods and goddesses with the vile One, she had lost the love-bond with the Mother herself—no better or worse than Anthea, for they'd both been paramount. She had forsaken everything she loved to save the Empire. And now, it had brought her all to ruin.

How fickle is fate. She thought of the augurs' beliefs on the Winds of Fortune. She wondered if it were true. Perhaps Animon, the Eagle Prince, would have understood Melorra's intentions, her desire to set things right. The Mother demanded forgiveness, but she did not forgive.

Child!

The word reverberated through her. The connection to the Mother surged to life, stronger than she'd ever remembered. It was as if the Mother lived within her, a part of her at least, and Melorra nearly fell off her horse.

Do not do anything rash. Wait here, on these cliffs. There are still things to be done.

The words of the Mother stopped. Still no sign of forgiveness. But regardless of it all, she would obey. She was a disciple of Lady Love unto death. She removed her shepherd's crook from her back and held it lengthwise, facing the endless waters of the sea. Her thoughts turned to summer, of the food and wine and laughter she had shared with Anthea her beloved. Now she had left this world, gone in body but not in the minds of the citizens. Their bond had broken, but she lived on in Melorra's mind.

A horn blew, loud and low, not an Imperial horn. She had a thought of running to meet it.

The Mother's voice filled her mind once again. *No. Do not. Wait.*

She turned her gaze back to the sea, crashing on the rocks far below. She waited.

CHAPTER FORTY-EIGHT:
SOUTH AND NORTH

Daimon Hierastos, Malleus

In his brown monk's habit, Claudian walked the Path of Tidus and the legions followed.

Some common citizens followed behind him as well, against Daimon's counsel, but he would not argue with an Adamantus. The enemy, now, was just a haze, but for miles around, men could see their handiwork: plumes of smoke rising into the cloudless sky, the burning buildings of Eximenius. Wherever the northmen barbarians went, destruction followed. They held nothing sacred, nothing beyond their looting hands. They stole the reliquary from Saint Loranna Temple— a priceless relic that held the woman's very bones—and melted it down into gold. It was clear they were demons in the flesh, more evil-hearted and more dangerous than the southrons had ever been. Claudian did not speak against them with the vitriol Daimon would have liked. But who was Daimon Malleus, paladin, to argue with the godsblood?

The burning buildings shone bronze on the barbarians' normally-pasty skin. A few of the horn-helmed warriors clutched severed heads in their arms. The mad-eyed berserkers were already roaring. *They will destroy us,* Daimon thought. But he calmed himself. Claudian would work another of his miracles like he had against the Redcloaks.

"I will s-speak to them!" Claudian walked out in front of them.

"Remember what happened last time?" Daimon did not doubt Claudian's divinity, but he couldn't let him act stupid. "The javelins—"

"Quiet," Claudian's firm, solemn command forced Daimon back into the proper reverence.

He said nothing more as Claudian walked forward.

"W-W-Wulfrik!"

At the stutter, a few barbarians laughed. *They will learn to respect the godsblood.* Daimon pursed his lips and sneered at their insolence.

"I w-wish to s-speak with your w-w-war ch-chief."

The laughing died down and silence reigned. Then the lines of warriors parted, and in their wake a giant walked forward. The war chief, Wulfrik, stood half again Claudian's height. In his hands, he clutched an axe that could chop a horse in two. *Thank Hieronus, Claudian is much quicker than a horse.*

"W-W-Wulfrik, I w-w-wish to ch-challenge y-you t-t-to a d-duel."

A few barbarians keeled over in laughter. Daimon shook his head.

Wulfrik snapped up his hand and hissed something in the barbarian tongue. Immediately, the laughing warriors stood upright, as if their leader threatened them with death. "Southlander," Wulfrik said in a harsh, guttural accent. "I tower above you. You know this will not end in your favor." He paused.

His blue eyes had none of the madness of the berserkers. *At least we can thank Hieronus for that.*

"What is your weapon?" Wulfrik snapped.

"I need no s-sword of steel," Claudian began. "I h-have a m-m-mind of st-steel, and th-the body of a-adamant."

Any laughs from the northmen stopped with Wulfrik's backward glare. He turned his ice-blue eyes back to Claudian. "And what are your terms?"

"If I win, you leave and call all your armies back to the north," Claudian said. "And if I lose, you will be crowned emperor."

The legionaries gave a few incredulous shouts, and Daimon bit his lip to prevent one of his own. *He knows what he is doing; he is a god,* Daimon told himself. Still, Daimon could not fathom a smelly, bearded northman sitting on the White Throne.

"I accept your challenge, southlander," Wulfrik growled. "It seems an unfair match but you have chosen your fate." The tower of a man carried his giant crescent-moon axe out into the paved road, where the god Claudian Adamantus waited for him.

"Domnir grant strength!" Wulfrik bellowed, and ran at him.

"H-Hieronus f-fight with me, th-the body of a-adamant!" Claudian answered him.

Wulfrik swung at Claudian, heaving the giant axe bit toward him. Claudian ducked out of the way and nailed Wulfrik with a kick that sent him stumbling backward. A legionary cheered; a few barbarians growled. Wulfrik's ice-blue eyes bulged, and a grimace formed on his pallid face.

Wulfrik pitched back his axe to try again.

The barbarians that had spears beat them into the dirt. Together, they began to chant:

Domnir, Domnir, Blue-Scaled Domnir!
You teach my hands to war, my soul to rage!
None can stand against your flame!
Domnir, Domnir, Blue-Scaled Domnir!

Wulfrik charged again, swinging his axe, and Claudian skirted out of the way in a twirl of brown cloth. Wulfrik charged again, and Claudian fell back easily. He assumed the scorpion stance once more, and Wulfrik's eyes narrowed.

The barbarians kept chanting. "Argh!" Wulfrik growled and charged Claudian once more. He swung again, harder than ever, but Claudian ducked underneath it and kicked Wulfrik so hard he went flying. His huge white fingers nearly lost grip on his axe.

"Kill him!" a legionary shouted. "Kill him, before he gets up."

But Claudian was backing away, eyeing Wulfrik as he stood to his feet, who looked winded with much of the vigor gone from his blue eyes. Still, he charged—sloppier this time, slower, a bit ambling—and Wulfrik heaved the axe at Claudian again in a sideways cross-cut.

Claudian leapt five feet in the air. *Impossible,* Daimon thought, *but he is an Adamantus.* In mid-leap he kicked Wulfrik in his huge jaw, and a tooth went flying. Wulfrik cried out and dropped his axe. When

Claudian landed once more, he drew back his fist and punched Wulfrik hard, despite the steel-plated armor of the war chiefs. His fist—as if of adamant—sundered steel and shattered Wulfrik's ribs with a sickening *crack!* The war chief hit the floor, lying on his side, not daring to take a breath.

The chanters went on, but their voices had lost vigor:

> *Domnir, Domnir, Blue-Scaled Domnir!*
> *You teach my hands to war, my soul to rage!*
> *None can stand against your flame!*
> *Domnir, Domnir, Blue-Scaled Domnir!*

"Kill me, then," the war chief rasped, each word obviously spoken at great pain. "I accept defeat. You are the better man."

"If y-you accept d-d-defeat, th-then I will g-give you mercy." Daimon wasn't so sure.

"If I was a coward, I would accept!" the war chief shouted through the pain. "Kill me and my men will go! The people of *Guthrekat* live by their word!"

"If it is w-what y-you wish, honorable n-northman," Claudian began, "th-then y-you shall g-get it. I w-wished to b-be allies, b-but… I s-shall answer your call." Claudian darted to the still body of Wulfrik and laid his adamant fingers on the neck; then he began to squeeze, and the neck crunched. Wulfrik's hands flailed, but he did not struggle. His men turned northward.

Daimon Hierastos thrust his warhammer high above his head. He was the first to cheer. *The battle is won,* he thought as the legions beat their swords against their shields and roared. *The battle is won by the godsblood, and the body of adamant.*

CHAPTER FIFTY-NINE: THE GOD RESTORED

Daimon Hierastos, Malleus

The Next Day…

The god Claudian sat on the White Throne. The Imperial Circlet gleamed on his thick, dark brown hair. All was as it should be. The Empire had found its rescue. The godsblood, the scion of the Adamanti, again ruled the world as was his right.

"Your Undying Glory!" Daimon approached him, feeling unworthy, as he well should. He fell to his knees. "An emperor deserves a wife fair and beautiful. Any woman in the Empire would be glad to have you as her mate."

Claudian shook his head. "I h-have taken a v-vow of c-chastity."

Ah, yes. Daimon remembered. The Monks Militant of Saint Traber was a celibate order. "Your Undying Glory, perhaps your vows can be forsaken for the good of the Empire."

"I w-will n-never forsake my v-vows," Claudian said.

Daimon thought through all the history he knew, and couldn't think of a time when a celibate monk served as emperor. There would be no heirs. The grandchildren by the demon Lysandra, perhaps. But to have a demoniac's blood in the Imperial line…

There had been childless emperors before. The line itself—with or without children—nearly always passed through adoption. It could be overcome. Grandmaster Cleon said the divinity descended not only through the blood, but also through the edict of the Adamanti.

His mission was done. In the coming weeks, he would board a ship and return to Imperiopoli to meet with the grandmaster. As a paladin, Daimon had much control over his own affairs. Though the

Pontifex did not allow his servants to worship the Adamanti or join the Imperial Cult, there was little chance of him finding out.

"Your Und—" A group of men in red hoods were appearing through the side doors. *Assassins.* Daimon swallowed a scream. They were running for the new emperor, poison-slicked daggers in their hands. They meant to kill him, he realized. They were Black Serpents, the deadliest of all assassins.

One leapt for him and struck, but Claudian ducked out of the way.

Even when he is not ready, he is ready.

One by one, Claudian struck them down. Like his father and the Adamanti before him, he overcame.

A good wind blows through the palace, a wind of Fortune, Daimon thought. *The god and his Empire have been restored.*

Through Redcloaks and heresies, through weak emperors and silver-tongues, through demoniacs and Black Serpents, the will of Imperium had prevailed.

The god and his Empire have been restored, and an Adamantus sits on the throne.

EPILOGUE

Melorra, Beloved of the Mother

Melorra watched waves crash against rocks, as she had done so often for the past day-and-a-half. The building heat of summer slicked her with sweat, and the azure robe she wore was too much to bear. But at noon, when the heat had become nearly unbearable, a welcome wind blew at her back; not a physical wind, or one an augur had called up. A spiritual wind, the presence of a friend she thought she'd lost.

Melorra turned around. The Revered Sister had left her horse a few yards away and now walked toward her. She lowered her white-hemmed blue hood and peered into Melorra's eyes.

"Revered One." Melorra dropped to one knee.

"I know what you've done, sister."

At the words, her eyes filled with tears. "I am sorry. There is nothing I can say."

"Do not be sorry. Any death is tragic, but you did what you had to do. I have communed with the Mother and she is displeased, but she has forgiven you. Even she knows you have done what had to be done. You have broken your oaths—"

Melorra sniffled and a tear ran down her cheek.

"—but I shall not excommunicate you. You are still a full sister. Melorra, you have done a difficult and unfortunate thing. But through your resolve, you have forestalled the world's destruction. The end is coming, Melorra. Not in my time or in yours. But despite Lidda's wicked heart, glimmers of truth are in her words. In my nightly communes, the Mother speaks candidly of the Red Mountain. We must all be vigilant. The massacre at Korthos, the shrines of Dol-Dagan…"

A shiver passed over Melorra at the name, and a cold wind blew.

"The first glimmers of shadow are spreading, Melorra. What will happen at the end, I do not know. All that is known, the Elders of the Far North have stowed away. The journey there is too far, at least for now."

The Elders. Most thought they were nothing more than a legend.

"I shall keep you on as a full sister, Melorra," she continued. "Your work is done in Imperial City. You have accomplished what was meant to be. You have lost a friend, a love-bond."

More tears streaked her cheeks.

"I want you in Amaroth. You have done well. The Mother does not like death, but she is pleased with your courage. The Grand Mother Temple beckons for you, my fellow sister. I hope you will heed our goddess' call. What say you?"

Memories flashed back to her of Anthea, her one true friend, the one who had passed away. She remembered her husband Claudio, the many years she spent within the Adamanti's household. Then she looked up into the Revered Sister's eyes and said, "Yes."

The two priestesses rode away on their horses, west down the road past the smoldering ruin of Eximenius. They rode as sisters in the palm of the Mother's hand, knowing full well that the end was coming soon.

GLOSSARY

CURRENCY

Aes: A copper coin, the cheapest unit of currency. Also called a copper or an "eagle."

Denar: A silver coin, worth twelve aesa. Also called a silver or a "moon."

Liber: A gold coin, worth eighty denara or approximately one-thousand aesa. Also called a gold, a "crown," or a "sovereign."

SURNAMES

No-Name: A general term for an infant left exposed after birth and taken in for adoption.

TERMS

Adamant: A metal of light bluish color. Its existence was known, but it could not be shaped until the eleventh century, when the Alchemist Collegium created a flame hot enough. The process of making adamant weapons is so expensive that hardly any can afford one outside of the upper tier of the military.

Amara: The goddess of motherly love.

Amaroth: A small temple city, the center of the priesthood of Amara.

Anthans: (1) Another name for Imperial City. (2) Anthans the Great, the last of the Sea Kings and the first emperor (having achieved the title with the ceding of Anthania).

Augusts: The higher of the two ruling classes (the other being Knights). They are the descendants of the original Peregothian families through the male line, and are the only people allowed to serve within the upper tier of the government.

Balzor: The god of death. His devotees are rumored to meet in secluded places and engage in ritual killings.

Barbarians: A general term for non-Imperials, both to the north and to the south.

Desolation, the: An area of intense fighting between Fharas and the Empire on the southern part of Khazidea. The constant burning and leveling of towns has turned this once-fertile region into a desert.

Empire, the: A large nation surrounding the Imperial Sea. Their flag is a gold war-eagle on a red field.

Elders, the: According to legend, a race of mystical beings rumored to live "beyond the reach of the north wind."

Eloesus: An ancient land famed for its wealth and rich culture. Since the 500s YE, an Imperial province. Their flag is a laurel-wreath on a green field.

Fharas: An ancient empire centered in the plain of Gor Ilán. Their flag is a golden four-pointed star on a purple field.

Gad: The northernmost and least populous province of the Empire, known for its light-featured inhabitants.

Haroon Spice: An intoxicant, currently banned in the Empire, which causes hallucinations and feelings of euphoria but—over the long term—afflicting the consumer with severe weight loss and, oftentimes, dementia. Crimson eyes are the telltale sign of long-term addicts.

Hieronus: The god of justice and just war.

Imperial City: Also called Anthans. The de facto capital of the Empire, and the largest city in the known world.

Imperial Council: A body of thirty Augusts (see above), given certain governmental powers, including the ability to remove the emperor. They are elected by the people of Imperial City across its thirty districts.

Imperial Cult: A group devoted to the worship of the emperors, especially the Adamanti, located in Imperiopoli.

Imperiopoli: A large city of Eloesus.

Imperium: The god of the Imperial state, represented as an eagle. His cult was founded in the 400s YE. The theologians of the Magisterium consider him a human invention.

Issa: Goddess of fertility. Worshiped mostly in Khazidea and the southlands, she nevertheless has a large temple in Imperiopoli.

Kernunnos: The wild god of forests, wildernesses, and changing seasons.

Korthos: An Eloesian metropolis.

Khazidea: A southern land along the Khazan River, surrounded by desert.

Kharn: The god of wrestling and physical strength.

Knight: (1) A mounted warrior, especially one wearing heavy armor; (2) A member of the lower tier of the Imperial upper class—the other being Augusts—officially tasked with the defense of the Empire. In actuality, not all knights serve actively as soldiers.

Lorenus: The god of the sea, favored by the city of Peregoth.

Magisterium, the: A large religious complex in Sanctum, led by the Pontifex, chief priest of Hieronus.

Malleus: An honorary title given to full-ranked paladins.

Monk: A member of a religious order. Monks Militant go to war, but are generally forbidden to shed blood; some wield clubs or maces to overcome this barrier, while others are sworn to use their fists.

Paradise Gardens: An elite enclave of the wealthy in the foothills of the Goldenhorn Mountains, a summer retreat popular with the August families of Imperial City.

Path of Tidus: A long paved road running from Imperial City to Zarubad far to the north.

Peregoth: The founding city of the Empire, built on an island of the same name.

Vestal: Generally, the Imperial equivalent of a nun in the north, a female monk.

Wall, the: A large wall separating the Empire from the northern barbarians. Its origins are a mystery.

IMPERIAL CITY MAP KEY

Suburro: An ancient, poor section of town, flanked by the Equine and Aurean Hills. Though widely known for its poverty and shanty homes, many great Imperials found their origins here.

West Side: Arguably part of the Suburro, a poor section of town predominating much of the western two-thirds of the city. It is filled with parks and spice dens.

a. **Armory District:** Once a center for the production of armaments and siege weaponry, this quiet district northeast of the Suburro is known for its charming shops and sprawling apartments.

b. **Kings Terrace:** An ancient enclave near the center of the city, featuring the mansions and homes of rich councilors and government officials. Most of these mansions cannot be bought and are passed down through families.

c. **Maxima:** Shops and theaters abound in this district, a center for drama and entertainment. Named for the war hero Adriano Maximus.

d. **Villa Regis:** A wealthy section of town, built along the shores of the North River.

e. **Bulus Wharf:** A section of town facing Imperial Harbor, a center of fishmongers and the fish trade.

Celsus Heights: A rich section of town built on a steep promontory. It is named for the infamous shipping magnate Celsus, who — rumor has it — burned down the area to build one of his mansions. Beside the rumor for arson, he was known for his unscrupulous business practices, charging exorbitant rents for those who stayed in his apartments, and was rumored to be a Strig, a kind of undead. Today, the mostly sumptuous apartment buildings overlook Imperial Harbor. Shops and music halls can also be found in abundance.

Harbor District: A sprawling district bordering the Imperial Harbor, featuring docks and warehouses.

Cloaca: The sewer district of Imperial City, flushing effluent into the South River. In ancient days, the first Cloaca broke and gushed forth water into the low-lying fields south of the river, creating the Palladian Swamp. The second Cloaca was built, much larger and stronger, after years of construction.

f.   **Market District:** A vast district predominating the center of the city, featuring its eponymous markets as well as slum areas.

g.   **Canyon Row:** Shops, apartments, temples and shrines predominate this central section of town. The Walk of Triumph begins here.

h.   **Newmarket:** A quiet district of shops and apartments.

i.   **Mud Bottom:** A dilapidated, ancient section of town, the most impoverished district.

Avediccus: A section of town facing the Palladian Swamp. Predominated by homes, shops, and small shrines, a concrete stairway into the swamp can be found here.

j.   **Meridia:** A section of town bordering the Palladian Swamp and city bounds, featuring apartment blocks, shops and administrative buildings.

k.   **Mystia:** A large section of town featuring markets, shops and homes, as well as the garrison for the city watch.

l.   **Villa Maris:** A section of town bordering the South River, highly developed, known for its taverns along the river's shore.

Emporia: Markets and shops predominate this central district.

m.   **Loud Surf:** A section of town built along cliffs, featuring often more pleasant weather than the city below. Its inhabitants call this section of town the city's most blessed area.

n.   **Perrine:** Named after the Emperor Perrius, this section of town has a mixture of wealth and poverty. It is a favored home for members of the military, as it connects to a road to Fort Mettius several miles away.

o. **Gaboline:** Named after the Emperor Gabolus, originally built around a fort then outside of city bounds, this district is known for its quaint stone streets and temples.

p. **West Limes:** A border area facing Wagontown Settlement, it is nonetheless highly developed and features vast theaters and gladiatorial arenas.

q. **East Limes:** A border area featuring many gladiatorial arenas. It abuts a section of cemeteries outside city bounds.

r. **Terrentian:** Named after the legate Terrentius, this section of town is known as a site of public executions. Shops and homes can be found here.

s. **Majorian Markets:** Named for two sprawling indoor market complexes, it is rumored that anything in Varda can be found here on sale.

The Ricci: A walled-off, closed section of town that houses the city's ratling population.

t. **The Strand:** A highly developed area of town known for its lighted roads, specialized taverns and bookshops.

u. **Meletus**: A section of apartments, shops and temples bordering the North River.

v. **Urubus**: A vast section of town below Celsus Heights, relatively impoverished, where the smoke of the city often settles. City administrators consider it a public health nuisance.

ABOUT THE AUTHOR

Cursed at birth with a wild imagination, Andrew Cooper spent his youth dreaming of worlds more exciting than Earth.

He is a graduate of the Odyssey Writing Workshop. His stories have appeared in Morpheus Tales, Fear and Trembling, Residential Aliens and Mindflights, among others.

Contact the Author

Visit **www.aj-cooper.com** to sign up for the newsletter and stay up-to-date on new releases.

Find him on Facebook at:

www.facebook.com/AJCooperauthor